Robert Browning, Elizabeth Barrett Browning

Last poems

Second Edition

Robert Browning, Elizabeth Barrett Browning

Last poems
Second Edition

ISBN/EAN: 9783337112820

Printed in Europe, USA, Canada, Australia, Japan

Cover: Foto ©Andreas Hilbeck / pixelio.de

More available books at **www.hansebooks.com**

LAST POEMS

BY

ELIZABETH BARRETT BROWNING.

Second Edition.

LONDON:

CHAPMAN AND HALL, 193, PICCADILLY.

1862.

PRINTED BY

JOHN EDWARD TAYLOR, LITTLE QUEEN STREET.

LINCOLN'S INN FIELDS.

TO " GRATEFUL FLORENCE,"

TO THE MUNICIPALITY, HER REPRESENTATIVE,

AND TO TOMMASEO, ITS SPOKESMAN,

MOST GRATEFULLY.

ADVERTISEMENT.

—— ◆ ——

THESE Poems are given as they occur on a list drawn up last June. A few had already been printed in periodicals.

There is hardly such direct warrant for publishing the Translations; which were only intended, many years ago, to accompany and explain certain Engravings after ancient Gems, in the projected work of a friend, by whose kindness they are now recovered: but as two of the original series (the 'Adonis' of Bion, and 'Song to the Rose' from Achilles Tatius) have subsequently appeared, it is presumed that the remainder may not improperly follow.

A single recent version is added.

LONDON, *February*, 1862.

CONTENTS.

—✦

b

TRANSLATIONS.

CONTENTS.

XI

LAST POEMS.

LITTLE MATTIE.

◆

I.

DEAD! Thirteen a month ago!
 Short and narrow her life's walk;
Lover's love she could not know
 Even by a dream or talk:
Too young to be glad of youth,
 Missing honour, labour, rest,
And the warmth of a babe's mouth
 At the blossom of her breast.
Must you pity her for this
And for all the loss it is,
You, her mother, with wet face,
Having had all in your case?

II.

Just so young but yesternight,
 Now she is as old as death.

Meek, obedient in your sight,
   Gentle to a beck or breath
Only on last Monday! Yours,
   Answering you like silver bells
Lightly touched! An hour matures:
   You can teach her nothing else.
She has seen the mystery hid
Under Egypt's pyramid:
By those eyelids pale and close
Now she knows what Rhamses knows.

III.

Cross her quiet hands, and smooth
   Down her patient locks of silk,
Cold and passive as in truth
   You your fingers in spilt milk
Drew along a marble floor;
   But her lips you cannot wring
Into saying a word more,
   'Yes,' or 'No,' or such a thing:
Though you call and beg and wreak
Half your soul out in a shriek,
She will lie there in default
And most innocent revolt.

IV.

Ay, and if she spoke, may be
   She would answer like the Son,
'What is now 'twixt thee and me?'
   Dreadful answer! better none.

Yours on Monday, God's to-day!
   Yours, your child, your blood, your heart,
Called . . you called her, did you say,
   'Little Mattie' for your part?
Now already it sounds strange,
And you wonder, in this change,
What He calls His angel-creature,
Higher up than you can reach her.

V.

'Twas a green and easy world
   As she took it; room to play,
(Though one's hair might get uncurled
   At the far end of the day).
What she suffered she shook off
   In the sunshine; what she sinned
She could pray on high enough
   To keep safe above the wind.
If reproved by God or you,
'Twas to better her, she knew;
And if crossed, she gathered still
'Twas to cross out something ill.

VI.

You, you had the right, you thought
   To survey her with sweet scorn,
Poor gay child, who had not caught
   Yet the octave-stretch forlorn
Of your larger wisdom! Nay,
   Now your places are changed so,

In that same superior way
　　She regards you dull and low
As you did herself exempt
From life's sorrows.　Grand contempt
Of the spirits risen awhile,
Who look back with such a smile!

VII.

There's the sting of't.　That, I think,
　　Hurts the most a thousandfold!
To feel sudden, at a wink,
　　Some dear child we used to scold,
Praise, love both ways, kiss and tease,
　　Teach and tumble as our own,
All its curls about our knees,
　　Rise up suddenly full-grown.
Who could wonder such a sight
Made a woman mad outright?
Show me Michael with the sword
Rather than such angels, Lord!

FALSE STEP.

I.

SWEET, thou hast trod on a heart.
　　Pass! there's a world full of men;
And women as fair as thou art
　　Must do such things now and then.

II.

Thou only hast stepped unaware,—
　　Malice, not one can impute;
And why should a heart have been there
　　In the way of a fair woman's foot?

III.

It was not a stone that could trip,
　　Nor was it a thorn that could rend:
Put up thy proud underlip!
　　'Twas merely the heart of a friend.

IV.

And yet peradventure one day
　　Thou, sitting alone at the glass,
Remarking the bloom gone away,
　　Where the smile in its dimplement was,

V.

And seeking around thee in vain
  From hundreds who flattered before,
Such a word as, 'Oh, not in the main
  Do I hold thee less precious, but more !' . .

VI.

Thou'lt sigh, very like, on thy part,
  'Of all I have known or can know,
I wish I had only that Heart
  I trod upon ages ago !'

VOID IN LAW.

— ◆ —

I.

Sleep, little babe, on my knee,
   Sleep, for the midnight is chill,
And the moon has died out in the tree,
   And the great human world goeth ill.
Sleep, for the wicked agree :
   Sleep, let them do as they will.
Sleep.

II.

Sleep, thou hast drawn from my breast
   The last drop of milk that was good ;
And now, in a dream, suck the rest,
   Lest the real should trouble thy blood.
Suck, little lips dispossessed,
   As we kiss in the air whom we would.
Sleep.

III.

O lips of thy father ! the same,
   So like ! Very deeply they swore
When he gave me his ring and his name,
   To take back, I imagined, no more !

And now is all changed like a game,
     Though the old cards are used as of yore?
Sleep.

IV.

'Void in law,' said the Courts. Something wrong
     In the forms? Yet, 'Till death part us two,
I, James, take thee, Jessie,' was strong,
     And ONE witness competent. True
Such a marriage was worth an old song,
     Heard in Heaven though, as plain as the New.
Sleep.

V.

Sleep, little child, his and mine!
     Her throat has the antelope curve,
And her cheek just the colour and line
     Which fade not before him nor swerve:
Yet *she* has no child!—the divine
     Seal of right upon loves that deserve.
Sleep.

VI.

My child! though the world take her part,
     Saying, 'She was the woman to choose,
He had eyes, was a man in his heart,'—
     We twain the decision refuse:
We .. weak as I am, as thou art, ..
     Cling on to him, never to loose.
Sleep.

VII.

He thinks that, when done with this place,
  All's ended? he'll new-stamp the ore?
Yes, Cæsar's—but not in our case.
  Let him learn we are waiting before
The grave's mouth, the heaven's gate, God's face,
  With implacable love evermore.
Sleep.

VIII.

He's ours, though he kissed her but now;
  He's ours, though she kissed in reply;
He's ours, though himself disavow,
  And God's universe favour the lie;
Ours to claim, ours to clasp, ours below,
  Ours above, . . if we live, if we die.
Sleep.

IX.

Ah baby, my baby, too rough
  Is my lullaby? What have I said?
Sleep! When I've wept long enough
  I shall learn to weep softly instead,
And piece with some alien stuff
  My heart to lie smooth for thy head.
Sleep.

X.

Two souls met upon thee, my sweet;
  Two loves led thee out to the sun:

Alas, pretty hands, pretty feet,
   If the one who remains (only one)
Set her grief at thee, turned in a heat
   To thine enemy,—were it well done?
Sleep.

XI.

May He of the manger stand near
   And love thee! An infant He came
To His own who rejected Him here,
   But the Magi brought gifts all the same.
I hurry the cross on my Dear!
   My gifts are the griefs I declaim!
Sleep.

LORD WALTER'S WIFE.

—◆—

I.

'But why do you go,' said the lady, while both sate under
the yew,

And her eyes were alive in their depth, as the kraken beneath the sea-blue.

II.

'Because I fear you,' he answered;—'because you are far
too fair,

And able to strangle my soul in a mesh of your gold-
coloured hair.'

III.

'Oh, that,' she said, 'is no reason! Such knots are quickly
undone,

And too much beauty, I reckon, is nothing but too much
sun.'

IV.

'Yet farewell so,' he answered;—'the sun-stroke's fatal at
times.

I value your husband, Lord Walter, whose gallop rings still
from the limes.'

V.

'Oh, that,' she said, 'is no reason. You smell a rose
    through a fence :
If two should smell it, what matter? who grumbles, and
    where's the pretence ?'

VI.

'But I,' he replied, 'have promised another, when love was
    free,
To love her alone, alone, who alone and afar loves me.'

VII.

'Why, that,' she said, 'is no reason. Love 's always free, I
    am told.
Will you vow to be safe from the headache on Tuesday, and
    think it will hold ?'

VIII.

'But you,' he replied, 'have a daughter, a young little
    child, who was laid
In your lap to be pure; so I leave you : the angels would
    make me afraid.'

IX.

'Oh, that,' she said, 'is no reason. The angels keep out
    of the way ;
And Dora, the child, observes nothing, although you should
    please me and stay.'

x.

At which he rose up in his anger,—'Why, now, you no
    longer are fair!
Why, now, you no longer are fatal, but ugly and hateful, I
    swear.'

xi.

At which she laughed out in her scorn.—'These men! Oh,
    these men overnice,
Who are shocked if a colour not virtuous, is frankly put
    on by a vice.'

xii.

Her eyes blazed upon him—'And *you!* You bring us
    your vices so near
That we smell them! You think in our presence a thought
    'twould defame us to hear!

xiii.

'What reason had you, and what right,—I appeal to your
    soul from my life,—
To find me too fair as a woman? Why, sir, I am pure, and
    a wife.

xiv.

'Is the day-star too fair up above you? It burns you not.
    Dare you imply
I brushed you more close than the star does, when Walter
    had set me as high?

XV.

'If a man finds a woman too fair, he means simply adapted
     too much
To uses unlawful and fatal. The praise!—shall I thank
     you for such?

XVI.

'Too fair?—not unless you misuse us! and surely if, once
     in a while,
You attain to it, straightway you call us no longer too fair,
     but too vile.

XVII.

'A moment,—I pray your attention!—I have a poor word
     in my head
I must utter, though womanly custom would set it down
     better unsaid.

XVIII.

'You grew, sir, pale to impertinence, once when I showed
     you a ring.
You kissed my fan when I dropped it. No matter!—I've
     broken the thing.

XIX.

'You did me the honour, perhaps, to be moved at my side
     now and then
In the senses—a vice, I have heard, which is common to
     beasts and some men.

XX.

'Love's a virtue for heroes!—as white as the snow on
  high hills,
And immortal as every great soul is that struggles, endures,
  and fulfils.

XXI.

'I love my Walter profoundly,—you, Maude, though you
  faltered a week,
For the sake of . . what was it? an eyebrow? or, less still,
  a mole on a cheek?

XXII.

'And since, when all's said, you're too noble to stoop to the
  frivolous cant
About crimes irresistible, virtues that swindle, betray and
  supplant,

XXIII.

'I determined to prove to yourself that, whate'er you might
  dream or avow
By illusion, you wanted precisely no more of me than you
  have now.

XXIV.

'There! Look me full in the face!—in the face. Under-
  stand, if you can,
That the eyes of such women as I am, are clean as the palm
  of a man.

XXV.

'Drop his hand, you insult him. Avoid us for fear we
     should cost you a scar—
You take us for harlots, I tell you, and not for the women
     we are.

XXVI.

'You wronged me: but then I considered . . . there's
     Walter! And so at the end,
I vowed that he should not be mulcted, by me, in the hand
     of a friend.

XXVII.

'Have I hurt you indeed? We are quits then. Nay, friend
     of my Walter, be mine!
Come Dora, my darling, my angel, and help me to ask him
     to dine.'

BIANCA AMONG THE NIGHTINGALES.

The cypress stood up like a church
    That night we felt our love would hold,
And saintly moonlight seemed to search
    And wash the whole world clean as gold;
The olives crystallized the vales'
    Broad slopes until the hills grew strong:
The fireflies and the nightingales
    Throbbed each to either, flame and song.
The nightingales, the nightingales.

II.

Upon the angle of its shade
    The cypress stood, self-balanced high;
Half up, half down, as double-made,
    Along the ground, against the sky.
And *we*, too! from such soul-height went
    Such leaps of blood, so blindly driven,
We scarce knew if our nature meant
    Most passionate earth or intense heaven.
The nightingales, the nightingales.

c

III.

We paled with love, we shook with love,
  We kissed so close we could not vow;
Till Giulio whispered, 'Sweet, above
  God's Ever guaranties this Now.'
And through his words the nightingales
  Drove straight and full their long clear call,
Like arrows through heroic mails,
  And love was awful in it all.
The nightingales, the nightingales.

IV.

O cold white moonlight of the north,
  Refresh these pulses, quench this hell!
O coverture of death drawn forth
  Across this garden-chamber . . well!
But what have nightingales to do
  In gloomy England, called the free . .
(Yes, free to die in ! . .) when we two
  Are sundered, singing still to me?
And still they sing, the nightingales.

V.

I think I hear him, how he cried
  'My own soul's life' between their notes.
Each man has but one soul supplied,
  And that's immortal. Though his throat's

On fire with passion now, to *her*
    He can't say what to me he said!
And yet he moves her, they aver.
    The nightingales sing through my head,
The nightingales, the nightingales.

VI.

He says to *her* what moves her most.
    He would not name his soul within
Her hearing,—rather pays her cost
    With praises to her lips and chin.
Man has but one soul, 'tis ordained,
    And each soul but one love, I add;
Yet souls are damned and love's profaned.
    These nightingales will sing me mad!
The nightingales, the nightingales.

VII.

I marvel how the birds can sing.
    There's little difference, in their view,
Betwixt our Tuscan trees that spring
    As vital flames into the blue,
And dull round blots of foliage meant
    Like saturated sponges here
To suck the fogs up.   As content
    Is *he* too in this land, 'tis clear.
And still they sing, the nightingales.

VIII.

My native Florence! dear, forgone!
    I see across the Alpine ridge
How the last feast-day of Saint John
    Shot rockets from Carraia bridge.
The luminous city, tall with fire,
    Trod deep down in that river of ours,
While many a boat with lamp and choir
    Skimmed birdlike over glittering towers.
I will not hear these nightingales.

IX.

I seem to float, *we* seem to float
    Down Arno's stream in festive guise;
A boat strikes flame into our boat,
    And up that lady seems to rise
As then she rose. The shock had flashed
    A vision on us! What a head,
What leaping eyeballs!—beauty dashed
    To splendour by a sudden dread.
And still they sing, the nightingales.

X.

Too bold to sin, too weak to die;
    Such women are so. As for me,
I would we had drowned there, he and I,
    That moment, loving perfectly.

He had not caught her with her loosed
    Gold ringlets . . rarer in the south . .
Nor heard the ' Grazie tanto ' bruised
    To sweetness by her English mouth.
And still they sing, the nightingales.

XI.

She had not reached him at my heart
    With her fine tongue, as snakes indeed
Kill flies; nor had I, for my part,
    Yearned after, in my desperate need,
And followed him as he did her
    To coasts left bitter by the tide,
Whose very nightingales, elsewhere
    Delighting, torture and deride!
For still they sing, the nightingales.

XII.

A worthless woman! mere cold clay
    As all false things are! but so fair,
She takes the breath of men away
    Who gaze upon her unaware.
I would not play her larcenous tricks
    To have her looks! She lied and stole,
And spat into my love's pure pyx
    The rank saliva of her soul.
And still they sing, the nightingales.

XIII.

I would not for her white and pink,
     Though such he likes—her grace of limb,
Though such he has praised—nor yet, I think,
     For life itself, though spent with him,
Commit such sacrilege, affront
     God's nature which is love, intrude
'Twixt two affianced souls, and hunt
     Like spiders, in the altar's wood.
I cannot bear these nightingales.

XIV.

If she chose sin, some gentler guise
     She might have sinned in, so it seems :
She might have pricked out both my eyes,
     And I still seen him in my dreams !
—Or drugged me in my soup or wine,
     Nor left me angry afterward :
To die here with his hand in mine
     His breath upon me, were not hard.
(Our Lady hush these nightingales !)

XV.

But set a springe for *him*, ' mio ben,'
     My only good, my first last love !—
Though Christ knows well what sin is, when
     He sees some things done they must move

Himself to wonder.   Let her pass.
　I think of her by night and day.
Must *I* too join her . . out, alas ! . .
　With Giulio, in each word I say ?
And evermore the nightingales !

XVI.

Giulio, my Giulio !—sing they so,
　And you be silent ? Do I speak,
And you not hear ? An arm you throw
　Round some one, and I feel so weak ?
—Oh, owl-like birds ! They sing for spite,
　They sing for hate, they sing for doom !
They'll sing through death who sing through night,
　They'll sing and stun me in the tomb—
The nightingales, the nightingales !

MY KATE.

I.

She was not as pretty as women I know,
And yet all your best made of sunshine and snow
Drop to shade, melt to nought in the long-trodden ways,
While she's still remembered on warm and cold days—
My Kate.

II.

Her air had a meaning, her movements a grace;
You turned from the fairest to gaze on her face:
And when you had once seen her forehead and mouth,
You saw as distinctly her soul and her truth—
My Kate.

III.

Such a blue inner light from her eyelids outbroke,
You looked at her silence and fancied she spoke:
When she did, so peculiar yet soft was the tone,
Though the loudest spoke also, you heard her alone—
My Kate.

IV.

I doubt if she said to you much that could act
As a thought or suggestion: she did not attract
In the sense of the brilliant or wise: I infer
'Twas her thinking of others, made you think of her—
My Kate.

V.

She never found fault with you, never implied
Your wrong by her right; and yet men at her side
Grew nobler, girls purer, as through the whole town
The children were gladder that pulled at her gown—
My Kate.

VI.

None knelt at her feet confessed lovers in thrall;
They knelt more to God than they used,—that was all:
If you praised her as charming, some asked what you meant,
But the charm of her presence was felt when she went—
My Kate.

VII.

The weak and the gentle, the ribald and rude,
She took as she found them, and did them all good;
It always was so with her--see what you have!
She has made the grass greener even here .. with her grave—
My Kate.

VIII.

My dear one!—when thou wast alive with the rest,
I held thee the sweetest and loved thee the best:
And now thou art dead, shall I not take thy part
As thy smiles used to do for thyself, my sweet Heart—
My Kate?

A SONG

FOR

THE RAGGED SCHOOLS OF LONDON.

WRITTEN IN ROME.

— ♦ —

I.

I AM listening here in Rome.
  'England's strong,' say many speakers,
'If she winks, the Czar must come,
  Prow and topsail, to the breakers.'

II.

'England's rich in coal and oak,'
  Adds a Roman, getting moody,
'If she shakes a travelling cloak,
  Down our Appian roll the scudi.'

III.

'England's righteous,' they rejoin,
  'Who shall grudge her exaltations,
When her wealth of golden coin
  Works the welfare of the nations?'

IV.

I am listening here in Rome.
    Over Alps a voice is sweeping—
'England's cruel! save us some
    Of these victims in her keeping!'

V.

As the cry beneath the wheel
    Of an old triumphal Roman
Cleft the people's shouts like steel,
    While the show was spoilt for no man,

VI.

Comes that voice.   Let others shout,
    Other poets praise my land here :
I am sadly sitting out,
    Praying, 'God forgive her grandeur.'

VII.

Shall we boast of empire, where
    Time with ruin sits commissioned?
In God's liberal blue air
    Peter's dome itself looks wizened ;

VIII.

And the mountains, in disdain,
    Gather back their lights of opal
From the dumb, despondent plain,
    Heaped with jawbones of a people.

IX.

Lordly English, think it o'er,
    Cæsar's doing is all undone!
You have cannons on your shore,
    And free parliaments in London,

X.

Princes' parks, and merchants' homes,
    Tents for soldiers, ships for seamen,—
Ay, but ruins worse than Rome's
    In your pauper men and women.

XI.

Women leering through the gas,
    (Just such bosoms used to nurse you)
Men, turned wolves by famine—pass!
    Those can speak themselves, and curse you.

XII.

But these others—children small,
    Spilt like blots about the city,
Quay, and street, and palace-wall—
    Take them up into your pity!

XIII.

Ragged children with bare feet,
    Whom the angels in white raiment
Know the names of, to repeat
    When they come on you for payment.

XIV.

Ragged children, hungry-eyed,
  Huddled up out of the coldness
On your doorsteps, side by side,
  Till your footman damns their boldness.

XV.

In the alleys, in the squares,
  Begging, lying little rebels;
In the noisy thoroughfares,
  Struggling on with piteous trebles.

XVI.

Patient children—think what pain
  Makes a young child patient—ponder!
Wronged too commonly to strain
  After right, or wish, or wonder.

XVII.

Wicked children, with peaked chins,
  And old foreheads! there are many
With no pleasures except sins,
  Gambling with a stolen penny.

XVIII.

Sickly children, that whine low
  To themselves and not their mothers,
From mere habit,—never so
  Hoping help or care from others.

XIX.

Healthy children, with those blue
    English eyes, fresh from their Maker,
Fierce and ravenous, staring through
    At the brown loaves of the baker.

XX.

I am listening here in Rome,
    And the Romans are confessing,
'English children pass in bloom
    All the prettiest made for blessing.

XXI.

' *Angli angeli!* ' (resumed
    From the mediæval story)
'Such rose angelhoods, emplumed
    In such ringlets of pure glory!'

XXII.

Can we smooth down the bright hair,
    O my sisters, calm, unthrilled in
Our heart's pulses? Can we bear
    The sweet looks of our own children,

XXIII.

While those others, lean and small,
    Scurf and mildew of the city,
Spot our streets, convict us all
    Till we take them into pity?

XXIV.

'Is it our fault?' you reply,
  'When, throughout civilization,
Every nation's empery
  Is asserted by starvation?

XXV.

'All these mouths we cannot feed,
  And we cannot clothe these bodies.'
Well, if man's so hard indeed,
  Let them learn at least what God is!

XXVI.

Little outcasts from life's fold,
  The grave's hope they may be joined in,
By Christ's covenant consoled
  For our social contract's grinding.

XXVII.

If no better can be done,
  Let us do but this,—endeavour
That the sun behind the sun
  Shine upon them while they shiver!

XXVIII.

On the dismal London flags,
  Through the cruel social juggle,
Put a thought beneath their rags
  To ennoble the heart's struggle.

XXIX.

O my sisters, not so much
  Are we asked for—not a blossom
From our children's nosegay, such
  As we gave it from our bosom,—

XXX.

Not the milk left in their cup,
  Not the lamp while they are sleeping,
Not the little cloak hung up
  While the coat's in daily keeping,—

XXXI.

But a place in RAGGED SCHOOLS,
  Where the outcasts may to-morrow
Learn by gentle words and rules
  Just the uses of their sorrow.

XXXII.

O my sisters! children small,
  Blue-eyed, wailing through the city—
Our own babes cry in them all:
  Let us take them into pity.

MAY'S LOVE.

—◆—

I.

You love all, you say,
  Round, beneath, above me :
Find me then some way
  Better than to love me,
Me, too, dearest May !

II.

O world-kissing eyes
  Which the blue heavens melt to !
I, sad, overwise,
  Loathe the sweet looks dealt to
All things—men and flies.

III.

You love all, you say :
  Therefore, Dear, abate me
Just your love, I pray !
  Shut your eyes and hate me—
Only *me*—fair May !

AMY'S CRUELTY.

——◆——

I.

FAIR Amy of the terraced house,
   Assist me to discover
Why you who would not hurt a mouse
   Can torture so your lover.

II.

You give your coffee to the cat,
   You stroke the dog for coming,
And all your face grows kinder at
   The little brown bee's humming.

III.

But when *he* haunts your door . . the town
   Marks coming and marks going . .
You seem to have stitched your eyelids down
   To that long piece of sewing!

IV.

You never give a look, not you,
    Nor drop him a 'Good morning,'
To keep his long day warm and blue,
    So fretted by your scorning.

V.

She shook her head—'The mouse and bee
    For crumb or flower will linger:
The dog is happy at my knee,
    The cat purrs at my finger.

VI.

'But *he* . . to *him*, the least thing given
    Means great things at a distance;
He wants my world, my sun, my heaven,
    Soul, body, whole existence.

VII.

'They say love gives as well as takes;
    But I'm a simple maiden,—
My mother's first smile when she wakes
    I still have smiled and prayed in.

VIII.

'I only know my mother's love
    Which gives all and asks nothing;
And this new loving sets the groove
    Too much the way of loathing.

IX.

'Unless he gives me all in change,
    I forfeit all things by him:
The risk is terrible and strange—
    I tremble, doubt, . . deny him.

X.

'He's sweetest friend, or hardest foe,
    Best angel, or worst devil;
I either hate or . . love him so,
    I can't be merely civil!

XI.

'You trust a woman who puts forth,
    Her blossoms thick as summer's?
You think she dreams what love is worth,
    Who casts it to new-comers?

XII.

'Such love's a cowslip-ball to fling,
    A moment's pretty pastime;
I give . . all me, if anything,
    The first time and the last time.

XIII.

'Dear neighbour of the trellised house,
    A man should murmur never,
Though treated worse than dog and mouse,
    Till doted on for ever!'

MY HEART AND I.

◆—

I.

Enough! we're tired, my heart and I.
  We sit beside the headstone thus,
  And wish that name were carved for us.
The moss reprints more tenderly
  The hard types of the mason's knife,
  As heaven's sweet life renews earth's life
With which we're tired, my heart and I.

II.

You see we're tired, my heart and I.
  We dealt with books, we trusted men,
  And in our own blood drenched the pen,
As if such colours could not fly.
  We walked too straight for fortune's end,
  We loved too true to keep a friend;
At last we're tired, my heart and I.

III.

How tired we feel, my heart and I!
  We seem of no use in the world;
  Our fancies hang grey and uncurled
About men's eyes indifferently;
  Our voice which thrilled you so, will let
  You sleep; our tears are only wet:
What do we here, my heart and I?

IV.

So tired, so tired, my heart and I!
  It was not thus in that old time
  When Ralph sat with me 'neath the lime
To watch the sunset from the sky.
  'Dear love, you're looking tired,' he said;
  I, smiling at him, shook my head:
'Tis now we're tired, my heart and I.

V.

So tired, so tired, my heart and I!
  Though now none takes me on his arm
  To fold me close and kiss me warm
Till each quick breath end in a sigh
  Of happy languor.   Now, alone,
  We lean upon this graveyard stone,
Uncheered, unkissed, my heart and I.

VI.

Tired out we are, my heart and I.
    Suppose the world brought diadems
    To tempt us, crusted with loose gems
Of powers and pleasures? Let it try.
    We scarcely care to look at even
    A pretty child, or God's blue heaven,
We feel so tired, my heart and I.

VII.

Yet who complains? My heart and I?
    In this abundant earth no doubt
    Is little room for things worn out:
Disdain them, break them, throw them by!
    And if before the days grew rough
    We *once* were loved, used,—well enough,
I think, we've fared, my heart and I.

THE BEST THING IN THE WORLD.

— ♦ —

WHAT's the best thing in the world?
June-rose, by May-dew impearled;
Sweet south-wind, that means no rain;
Truth, not cruel to a friend;
Pleasure, not in haste to end;
Beauty, not self-decked and curled
Till its pride is over-plain;
Light, that never makes you wink;
Memory, that gives no pain;
Love, when, *so*, you're loved again.
What's the best thing in the world?
—Something out of it, I think.

WHERE'S AGNES?

I.

Nay, if I had come back so,
  And found her dead in her grave,
And if a friend I know
  Had said, ' Be strong, nor rave :
She lies there, dead below :

II.

' I saw her, I who speak,
  White, stiff, the face one blank :
The blue shade came to her cheek
  Before they nailed the plank,
For she had been dead a week.'

III.

Why, if he had spoken so,
  I might have believed the thing,
Although her look, although
  Her step, laugh, voice's ring
Lived in me still as they do.

IV.

But dead that other way,
  Corrupted thus and lost?
That sort of worm in the clay?
  I cannot count the cost,
That I should rise and pay.

V.

My Agnes false? such shame?
  She? Rather be it said
That the pure saint of her name
  Has stood there in her stead,
And tricked you to this blame.

VI.

Her very gown, her cloak
  Fell chastely: no disguise,
But expression! while she broke
  With her clear grey morning-eyes
Full upon me and then spoke.

VII.

She wore her hair away
  From her forehead,—like a cloud
Which a little wind in May
  Peels off finely: disallowed
Though bright enough to stay.

VIII.

For the heavens must have the place
  To themselves, to use and shine in,
As her soul would have her face
  To press through upon mine, in
That orb of angel grace.

IX.

Had she any fault at all,
  'Twas having none, I thought too—
There seemed a sort of thrall;
  As she felt her shadow ought to
Fall straight upon the wall.

X.

Her sweetness strained the sense
  Of common life and duty;
And every day's expense
  Of moving in such beauty
Required, almost, defence.

XI.

What good, I thought, is done
  By such sweet things, if any?
This world smells ill i' the sun
  Though the garden-flowers are many,—
She is only one.

XII.

Can a voice so low and soft
   Take open actual part
With Right,—maintain aloft
   Pure truth in life or art,
Vexed always, wounded oft?—

XIII.

She fit, with that fair pose
   Which melts from curve to curve,
To stand, run, work with those
   Who wrestle and deserve,
And speak plain without glose?

XIV.

But I turned round on my fear
   Defiant, disagreeing—
What if God has set her here
   Less for action than for Being?—
For the eye and for the ear.

XV.

Just to show what beauty may,
   Just to prove what music can,—
And then to die away
   From the presence of a man,
Who shall learn, henceforth, to pray?

XVI.

As a door, left half ajar
    In heaven, would make him think
How heavenly-different are
    Things glanced at through the chink,
Till he pined from near to far.

XVII.

That door could lead to hell?
    That shining merely meant
Damnation? What! She fell
    Like a woman, who was sent
Like an angel, by a spell?

XVIII.

She, who scarcely trod the earth,
    Turned mere dirt? My Agnes,—mine!
Called so! felt of too much worth
    To be used so! too divine
To be breathed near, and so forth!

XIX.

Why, I dared not name a sin
    In her presence: I went round,
Clipped its name and shut it in
    Some mysterious crystal sound,—
Changed the dagger for the pin.

XX.

Now you name herself *that word?*
 O my Agnes! O my saint!
Then the great joys of the Lord
 Do not last? Then all this paint
Runs off nature? leaves a board?

XXI.

Who's dead here? No, not she:
 Rather I! or whence this damp
Cold corruption's misery?
 While my very mourners stamp
Closer in the clods on me.

XXII.

And my mouth is full of dust
 Till I cannot speak and curse—
Speak and damn him . . 'Blame's unjust'?
 Sin blots out the universe,
All because she would and must?

XXIII.

She, my white rose, dropping off
 The high rose-tree branch! and not
That the night-wind blew too rough,
 Or the noon-sun burnt too hot,
But, that being a rose—'twas enough!

XXIV.

Then henceforth, may earth grow trees !
    No more roses !—hard straight lines
To score lies out ! none of these
    Fluctuant curves ! but firs and pines,
Poplars, cedars, cypresses !

DE PROFUNDIS.

———◆———

I.

THE face which, duly as the sun,
Rose up for me with life begun,
To mark all bright hours of the day
With hourly love, is dimmed away,—
And yet my days go on, go on.

II.

The tongue which, like a stream, could run
Smooth music from the roughest stone,
And every morning with 'Good day'
Make each day good, is hushed away,—
And yet my days go on, go on.

III.

The heart which, like a staff, was one
For mine to lean and rest upon,
The strongest on the longest day
With steadfast love, is caught away,—
And yet my days go on, go on.

IV.

And cold before my summer's done,
And deaf in Nature's general tune,
And fallen too low for special fear,
And here, with hope no longer here,—
While the tears drop, my days go on.

V.

The world goes whispering to its own,
'This anguish pierces to the bone;'
And tender friends go sighing round,
'What love can ever cure this wound?'
My days go on, my days go on.

VI.

The past rolls forward on the sun
And makes all night. O dreams begun,
Not to be ended! Ended bliss,
And life that will not end in this!
My days go on, my days go on.

VII.

Breath freezes on my lips to moan:
As one alone, once not alone,
I sit and knock at Nature's door,
Heart-bare, heart-hungry, very poor,
Whose desolated days go on.

E

VIII.

I knock and cry,—Undone, undone!
Is there no help, no comfort,—none?
No gleaning in the wide wheat-plains
Where others drive their loaded wains?
My vacant days go on, go on.

IX.

This Nature, though the snows be down,
Thinks kindly of the bird of June:
The little red hip on the tree
Is ripe for such. What is for me,
Whose days so winterly go on?

X.

No bird am I, to sing in June,
And dare not ask an equal boon.
Good nests and berries red are Nature's
To give away to better creatures,—
And yet my days go on, go on.

XI.

I ask less kindness to be done,—
Only to loose these pilgrim-shoon,
(Too early worn and grimed) with sweet
Cool deathly touch to these tired feet,
Till days go out which now go on.

XII.

Only to lift the turf unmown
From off the earth where it has grown,
Some cubit-space, and say, ' Behold,
Creep in, poor Heart, beneath that fold,
Forgetting how the days go on.'

XIII.

What harm would that do? Green anon
The sward would quicken, overshone
By skies as blue; and crickets might
Have leave to chirp there day and night
While my new rest went on, went on.

XIV.

From gracious Nature have I won
Such liberal bounty? may I run
So, lizard-like, within her side,
And there be safe, who now am tried
By days that painfully go on?

XV.

—A Voice reproves me thereupon,
More sweet than Nature's when the drone
Of bees is sweetest, and more deep
Than when the rivers overleap
The shuddering pines, and thunder on.

E 2

XVI.

God's Voice, not Nature's! Night and noon
He sits upon the great white throne
And listens for the creatures' praise.
What babble we of days and days?
The Day-spring He, whose days go on.

XVII.

He reigns above, He reigns alone;
Systems burn out and leave His throne:
Fair mists of seraphs melt and fall
Around Him, changeless amid all,—
Ancient of Days, whose days go on.

XVIII.

He reigns below, He reigns alone,
And, having life in love forgone
Beneath the crown of sovran thorns,
He reigns the Jealous God. Who mourns
Or rules with Him, while days go on?

XIX.

By anguish which made pale the sun,
I hear Him charge His saints that none
Among His creatures anywhere
Blaspheme against Him with despair,
However darkly days go on.

XX.

Take from my head the thorn-wreath brown!
No mortal grief deserves that crown.
O súpreme Love, chief Misery,
The sharp regalia are for THEE
Whose days eternally go on!

XXI.

For us,—whatever's undergone,
Thou knowest, willest what is done.
Grief may be joy misunderstood;
Only the Good discerns the good.
I trust Thee while my days go on.

XXII.

Whatever's lost, it first was won:
We will not struggle nor impugn.
Perhaps the cup was broken here,
That Heaven's new wine might show more clear.
I praise Thee while my days go on.

XXIII.

I praise Thee while my days go on;
I love Thee while my days go on:
Through dark and dearth, through fire and frost,
With emptied arms and treasure lost,
I thank Thee while my days go on.

XXIV.

And having in Thy life-depth thrown
Being and suffering (which are one),
As a child drops his pebble small
Down some deep well, and hears it fall
Smiling—so I. THY DAYS GO ON.

A MUSICAL INSTRUMENT.

I.

WHAT was he doing, the great god Pan,
　Down in the reeds by the river?
Spreading ruin and scattering ban,
Splashing and paddling with hoofs of a goat,
And breaking the golden lilies afloat
　With the dragon-fly on the river.

II.

He tore out a reed, the great god Pan,
　From the deep cool bed of the river:
The limpid water turbidly ran,
And the broken lilies a-dying lay,
And the dragon-fly had fled away,
　Ere he brought it out of the river.

III.

High on the shore sate the great god Pan,
　While turbidly flowed the river;
And hacked and hewed as a great god can,
With his hard bleak steel at the patient reed,
Till there was not a sign of a leaf indeed
　To prove it fresh from the river.

IV.

He cut it short, did the great god Pan,
  (How tall it stood in the river!)
Then drew the pith, like the heart of a man,
Steadily from the outside ring,
And notched the poor dry empty thing
  In holes, as he sate by the river.

V.

'This is the way,' laughed the great god Pan,
  (Laughed while he sate by the river,)
'The only way, since gods began
To make sweet music, they could succeed.'
Then, dropping his mouth to a hole in the reed,
  He blew in power by the river.

VI.

Sweet, sweet, sweet, O Pan!
  Piercing sweet by the river!
Blinding sweet, O great god Pan!
The sun on the hill forgot to die,
And the lilies revived, and the dragon-fly
  Came back to dream on the river.

VII.

Yet half a beast is the great god Pan,
  To laugh as he sits by the river,
Making a poet out of a man:
The true gods sigh for the cost and pain,—
For the reed which grows nevermore again
  As a reed with the reeds in the river.

FIRST NEWS FROM VILLAFRANCA.

I.

Peace, peace, peace, do you say?
 What!—with the enemy's guns in our ears?
 With the country's wrong not rendered back?
What!—while Austria stands at bay
 In Mantua, and our Venice bears
 The cursed flag of the yellow and black?

II.

Peace, peace, peace, do you say?
 And this the Mincio?   Where's the fleet,
 And where's the sea?   Are we all blind
Or mad with the blood shed yesterday,
 Ignoring Italy under our feet,
 And seeing things before, behind?

III.

Peace, peace, peace, do you say?
 What!—uncontested, undenied?
 Because we triumph, we succumb?
A pair of Emperors stand in the way,
 (One of whom is a man, beside)
To sign and seal our cannons dumb?

IV.

No, not Napoleon !—he who mused
    At Paris, and at Milan spake,
    And at Solferino led the fight :
Not he we trusted, honoured, used
    Our hopes and hearts for . . till they break—
    Even so, you tell us . . in his sight.

V.

Peace, peace, is still your word ?
    We say you lie then !—that is plain.
    There *is* no peace, and shall be none.
Our very Dead would cry ' Absurd !'
    And clamour that they died in vain,
    And whine to come back to the sun.

VI.

Hush ! more reverence for the Dead !
    They've done the most for Italy
    Evermore since the earth was fair.
Now would that *we* had died instead,
    Still dreaming peace meant liberty,
    And did not, could not mean despair.

VII.

Peace, you say ?—yes, peace, in truth !
    But such a peace as the car can achieve
    'Twixt the rifle's click and the rush of the ball,
'Twixt the tiger's spring and the crunch of the tooth,
    'Twixt the dying atheist's negative
    And God's Face—waiting, after all !

KING VICTOR EMANUEL ENTERING FLORENCE, APRIL, 1860.

I.

KING of us all, we cried to thee, cried to thee,
  Trampled to earth by the beasts impure,
  Dragged by the chariots which shame as they roll:
The dust of our torment far and wide to thee
  Went up, dark'ning thy royal soul.
      Be witness, Cavour,
That the King was sad for the people in thrall,
      This King of us all!

II.

King, we cried to thee! Strong in replying,
  Thy word and thy sword sprang rapid and sure,
  Cleaving our way to a nation's place.
Oh, first soldier of Italy!—crying
  Now grateful, exultant, we look in thy face.
      Be witness, Cavour,
That, freedom's first soldier, the freed should call
      First King of them all!

III.

This is our beautiful Italy's birthday ;
    High-thoughted souls, whether many or fewer,
    Bring her the gift, and wish her the good,
While Heaven presents on this sunny earth-day
    The noble king to the land renewed :
        Be witness, Cavour !
Roar, cannon-mouths !   Proclaim, install
      The King of us all !

IV.

Grave he rides through the Florence gateway,
    Clenching his face into calm, to immure
    His struggling heart till it half disappears ;
If he relaxed for a moment, straightway
    He would break out into passionate tears—
        (Be witness, Cavour !)
While rings the cry without interval,
      "Live, King of us all !"

V.

Cry, free peoples !   Honour the nation
    By crowning the true man—and none is truer :
    Pisa is here, and Livorno is here,
And thousands of faces, in wild exultation,
    Burn over the windows to feel him near—
        (Be witness, Cavour !)
Burn over from terrace, roof, window and wall,
      On this King of us all.

VI.

Grave!   A good man's ever the graver
    For bearing a nation's trust secure;
    And *he*, he thinks of the Heart, beside,
Which broke for Italy, failing to save her,
    And pining away by Oporto's tide:
        Be witness, Cavour,
That he thinks of his vow on that royal pall,
        This King of us all.

VII.

Flowers, flowers, from the flowery city!
    Such innocent thanks for a deed so pure,
    As, melting away for joy into flowers,
The nation invites him to enter his Pitti
    And evermore reign in this Florence of ours.
        Be witness, Cavour!
He'll stand where the reptiles were used to crawl,
        This King of us all.

VIII.

Grave, as the manner of noble men is—
    Deeds unfinished will weigh on the doer:
    And, baring his head to those crape-veiled flags,
He bows to the grief of the South and Venice.
    Oh, riddle the last of the yellow to rags,
        And swear by Cavour
That the King shall reign where the tyrants fall,
        True King of us all!

THE SWORD OF CASTRUCCIO CASTRACANI.

" Questa è per me."—KING VICTOR EMANUEL.

—◆—

I.

WHEN Victor Emanuel the King,
  Went down to his Lucca that day,
The people, each vaunting the thing
  As he gave it, gave all things away,—
  In   burst of fierce gratitude, say,
As they tore out their hearts for the king.

II.

—Gave the green forest-walk on the wall,
  With the Apennine blue through the trees ;
Gave the palaces, churches, and all
  The great pictures which burn out of these :
  But the eyes of the King seemed to freeze
As he glanced upon ceiling and wall.

III.

"Good," said the King as he passed.
　　Was he cold to the arts?—or else coy
To possession? or crossed, at the last,
　　(Whispered some) by the vote in Savoy?
　　Shout! Love him enough for his joy!
"Good," said the King as he passed.

IV.

He, travelling the whole day through flowers
　　And protesting amenities, found
At Pistoia, betwixt the two showers
　　Of red roses, the 'Orphans,' (renowned
　　As the heirs of Puccini) who wound
With a sword through the crowd and the flowers.

V.

"'Tis the sword of Castruccio, O King,—
　　In that strife of intestinal hate,
Very famous! Accept what we bring,
　　We who cannot be sons, by our fate,
　　Rendered citizens by thee of late,
And endowed with a country and king.

VI.

"Read! Puccini has willed that this sword
　　(Which once made in an ignorant feud
Many orphans) remain in our ward
　　Till some patriot its pure civic blood
　　Wipe away in the foe's and make good,
In delivering the land by the sword."

VII.

Then the King exclaimed, " This is for *me !* "
 And he dashed out his hand on the hilt,
While his blue eye shot fire openly,
 And his heart overboiled till it spilt
 A hot prayer,—" God ! the rest as Thou wilt !
But grant me this !—*This* is for *me.*"

VIII.

O Victor Emanuel, the King,
 The sword be for *thee*, and the deed,
And nought for the alien, next spring,
 Nought for Hapsburg and Bourbon agreed—
 But, for us, a great Italy freed,
With a hero to head us,—our King !

SUMMING UP IN ITALY.

(INSCRIBED TO INTELLIGENT PUBLICS OUT OF IT.)

— ♦ —

I.

OBSERVE how it will be at last,
  When our Italy stands at full stature,
A year ago tied down so fast
  That the cord cut the quick of her nature!
You'll honour the deed and its scope,
  Then, in logical sequence upon it,
Will use up the remnants of rope
  By hanging the men who have done it.

II.

The speech in the Commons, which hits you
  A sketch off, how dungeons must feel,—
The official despatch, which commits you
  From stamping out groans with your heel,—
Suggestions in journal or book for
  Good efforts,—are praised as is meet:
But what in this world can men look for,
  Who only achieve and complete?

F

III.

True, you've praise for the fireman who sets his
    Brave face to the axe of the flame,
Disappears in the smoke, and then fetches
    A babe down, or idiot that's lame,—
For the boor even, who rescues through pity
    A sheep from the brute who would kick it:
But saviours of nations!—'tis pretty,
    And doubtful : they *may* be so wicked :

IV.

Azeglio, Farini, Mamiani,
    Ricasoli,—doubt by the dozen !—here's
Pepoli too, and Cipriani,
    Imperial cousins and cozeners—
Arese, Laiatico,—courtly
    Of manners, if stringent of mouth :
Garibaldi ! we'll come to him shortly,
    (As soon as he *ends* in the South).

V.

Napoleon—as strong as ten armies,
    Corrupt as seven devils—a fact
You accede to, then seek where the harm is
    Drained off from the man to his act,
And find—a free nation ! Suppose
    Some hell-brood in Eden's sweet greenery,
Convoked for creating—a rose !
    Would it suit the infernal machinery ?

VI.

Cavour,—to the despot's desire,
  Who his own thought so craftily marries—
What is he but just a thin wire
  For conducting the lightning from Paris?
Yes, write down the two as compeers,
  Confessing (you would not permit a lie)
He bore up his Piedmont ten years
  Till she suddenly smiled and was Italy.

VII.

And the King, with that 'stain on his scutcheon,'*
  Savoy—as the calumny runs ;
(If it be not his blood,—with his clutch on
  The sword, and his face to the guns.)
O first, where the battle-storm gathers,
  O loyal of heart on the throne,
Let those keep the ' graves of their fathers,'
  Who quail, in a nerve, from their own !

VIII.

For *thee*—through the dim Hades-portal
  The dream of a voice—' Blessed thou
' Who hast made all thy race twice immortal !
  ' No need of the sepulchres now !
—' Left to Bourbons and Hapsburgs, who fester
  ' Above-ground with worm-eaten souls,
' While the ghost of some pale feudal jester
  ' Before them strews treaties in holes.'

  * Blue Book. Diplomatical Correspondence.

IX.

But hush !—am I dreaming a poem
    Of Hades, Heaven, Justice ?   Not I—
I began too far off, in my proem,
    With what men believe and deny :
And on earth, whatsoever the need is,
    (To sum up as thoughtful reviewers)
The moral of every great deed is
    The virtue of slandering the doers.

"DIED . . ."

(The 'Times' Obituary.)

— ♦

I.

WHAT shall we add now?   He is dead.
And I who praise and you who blame,
With wash of words across his name,
Find suddenly declared instead—
'On Sunday, third of August, dead.'

II.

Which stops the whole we talked today.
I, quickened to a plausive glance
At his large general tolerance
By common people's narrow way,
Stopped short in praising.   Dead, they say.

III.

And you, who had just put in a sort
Of cold deduction—"rather, large
Through weakness of the continent marge,
Than greatness of the thing contained"—
Broke off.   Dead!—there, you stood restrained.

IV.

As if we had talked in following one
   Up some long gallery. 'Would you choose
   An air like that? The gait is loose—
Or noble.' Sudden in the sun
An oubliette winks. Where *is* he? Gone.

V.

Dead. Man's ' I was' by God's ' I am '—
   All hero-worship comes to that.
   High heart, high thought, high fame, as flat
As a gravestone. Bring your *Jacet jam*—
The epitaph 's an epigram.

VI.

Dead. There 's an answer to arrest
   All carping. Dust 's his natural place?
   He 'll let the flies buzz round his face
And, though you slander, not protest?
—From such an one, exact the Best?

VII.

Opinions gold or brass are null.
   We chuck our flattery or abuse,
   Called Cæsar's due, as Charon's dues,
I' the teeth of some dead sage or fool,
To mend the grinning of a skull.

VIII.

Be abstinent in praise and blame.
   The man's still mortal, who stands first,
   And mortal only, if last and worst.
Then slowly lift so frail a fame,
Or softly drop so poor a shame.

THE FORCED RECRUIT.

SOLFERINO, 1859.

—◆—

I.

In the ranks of the Austrian you found him,
 He died with his face to you all;
Yet bury him here where around him
 You honour your bravest that fall.

II.

Venetian, fair-featured and slender,
 He lies shot to death in his youth,
With a smile on his lips over-tender
 For any mere soldier's dead mouth.

III.

No stranger, and yet not a traitor,
 Though alien the cloth on his breast,
Underneath it how seldom a greater
 Young heart, has a shot sent to rest!

IV.

By your enemy tortured and goaded
    To march with them, stand in their file,
His musket (see) never was loaded,
    He facing your guns with that smile!

v.

As orphans yearn on to their mothers,
    He yearned to your patriot bands;—
'Let me die for our Italy, brothers,
    If not in your ranks, by your hands!

VI.

'Aim straightly, fire steadily! spare me
    A ball in the body which may
Deliver my heart here, and tear me
    This badge of the Austrian away!'

VII.

So thought he, so died he this morning.
    What then? many others have died.
Ay, but easy for men to die scorning
    The death-stroke, who fought side by side—

VIII.

One tricolour floating above them;
    Struck down 'mid triumphant acclaims
Of an Italy rescued to love them
    And blazon the brass with their names.

IX.

But he,—without witness or honour,
    Mixed, shamed in his country's regard,
With the tyrants who march in upon her,
    Died faithful and passive : 'twas hard.

X.

'Twas sublime.   In a cruel restriction
    Cut off from the guerdon of sons,
With most filial obedience, conviction,
    His soul kissed the lips of her guns.

XI.

That moves you ? Nay, grudge not to show it,
    While digging a grave for him here :
The others who died, says your poet,
    Have glory,—let *him* have a tear.

GARIBALDI.

—◆—

I.

HE bent his head upon his breast
  Wherein his lion-heart lay sick :—
  'Perhaps we are not ill-repaid ;
Perhaps this is not a true test ;
  Perhaps that was not a foul trick ;
  Perhaps none wronged, and none betrayed.

II.

'Perhaps the people's vote which here
  United, there may disunite,
  And both be lawful as they think ;
Perhaps a patriot statesman, dear
  For chartering nations, can with right
  Disfranchise those who hold the ink.

III.

'Perhaps men's wisdom is not craft ;
  Men's greatness, not a selfish greed ;
  Men's justice, not the safer side ;
Perhaps even women, when they laughed,
  Wept, thanked us that the land was freed,
  Not wholly (though they kissed us) lied.

IV.

'Perhaps no more than this we meant,
  When up at Austria's guns we flew,
  And quenched them with a cry apiece,
Italia !—Yet a dream was sent . .
  The little house my father knew,
  The olives and the palms of Nice.'

V.

He paused, and drew his sword out slow,
  Then pored upon the blade intent,
  As if to read some written thing;
While many murmured,—'He will go
  In that despairing sentiment
  And break his sword before the King.'

VI.

He poring still upon the blade,
  His large lid quivered, something fell.
  'Perhaps,' he said, 'I was not born
With such fine brains to treat and trade,—
  And if a woman knew it well,
  Her falsehood only meant her scorn.

VII.

'Yet through Varese's cannon-smoke
  My eye saw clear: men feared this man
  At Como, where this sword could seal
Death's protocol with every stroke:
  And now . . the drop there scarcely can
  Impair the keenness of the steel.

VIII.

So man and sword may have their use;
   And if the soil beneath my foot
   In valour's act is forfeited,
I'll strike the harder, take my dues
   Out nobler, and all loss confute
   From ampler heavens above my head.

IX.

'My King, King Victor, I am thine!
   So much Nice-dust as what I am
   (To make our Italy) must cleave.
Forgive that.' Forward with a sign
   He went.

           You've seen the telegram?
   Palermo's taken, we believe.

ONLY A CURL.

— ◆ —

I.

FRIENDS of faces unknown and a land
   Unvisited over the sea,
Who tell me how lonely you stand
With a single gold curl in the hand
   Held up to be looked at by me,—

II.

While you ask me to ponder and say
   What a father and mother can do,
With the bright fellow-locks put away
Out of reach, beyond kiss, in the clay
   Where the violets press nearer than you.

III.

Shall I speak like a poet, or run
   Into weak woman's tears for relief?
Oh, children!—I never lost one,—
Yet my arm 's round my own little son,
   And Love knows the secret of Grief.

IV.

And I feel what it must be and is,
   When God draws a new angel so
Through the house of a man up to His,
With a murmur of music, you miss,
   And a rapture of light, you forgo.

V.

How you think, staring on at the door,
   Where the face of your angel flashed in,
That its brightness, familiar before,
Burns off from you ever the more
   For the dark of your sorrow and sin.

VI.

'God lent him and takes him,' you sigh;
   —Nay, there let me break with your pain:
God's generous in giving, say I,—
And the thing which He gives, I deny
   That He ever can take back again.

VII.

He gives what He gives. I appeal
   To all who bear babes—in the hour
When the veil of the body we feel
Rent round us,—while torments reveal
   The motherhood's advent in power,

VIII.

And the babe cries!—has each of us known
   By apocalypse (God being there
Full in nature) the child is our own,
Life of life, love of love, moan of moan,
   Through all changes, all times, everywhere.

IX.

He's ours and for ever.   Believe,
   O father!—O mother, look back
To the first love's assurance.   To give
Means with God not to tempt or deceive
   With a cup thrust in Benjamin's sack.

X.

He gives what He gives.   Be content!
   He resumes nothing given,—be sure!
God lend? Where the usurers lent
In His temple, indignant He went
   And scourged away all those impure.

XI.

He lends not; but gives to the end,
   As He loves to the end. If it seem
That He draws back a gift, comprehend
'Tis to add to it rather,—amend,
   And finish it up to your dream,—

XII.

Or keep,—as a mother will toys
  Too costly, though given by herself,
Till the room shall be stiller from noise,
And the children more fit for such joys,
  Kept over their heads on the shelf.

XIII.

So look up, friends! you, who indeed
  Have possessed in your house a sweet piece
Of the Heaven which men strive for, must need
Be more earnest than others are,—speed
  Where they loiter, persist where they cease.

XIV.

You know how one angel smiles there.
  Then weep not. 'Tis easy for you
To be drawn by a single gold hair
Of that curl, from earth's storm and despair,
  To the safe place above us.   Adieu.

A VIEW ACROSS THE ROMAN CAMPAGNA.

1861.

— ✦ —

I.

OVER the dumb Campagna-sea,
  Out in the offing through mist and rain,
Saint Peter's Church heaves silently
  Like a mighty ship in pain,
  Facing the tempest with struggle and strain.

II.

Motionless waifs of ruined towers,
  Soundless breakers of desolate land :
The sullen surf of the mist devours
  That mountain-range upon either hand,
  Eaten away from its outline grand.

III.

And over the dumb Campagna-sea
  Where the ship of the Church heaves on to wreck,
Alone and silent as God must be,
  The Christ walks.   Ay, but Peter's neck
  Is stiff to turn on the foundering deck.

IV.

Peter, Peter! if such be thy name,
　Now leave the ship for another to steer,
And proving thy faith evermore the same,
　Come forth, tread out through the dark and drear,
　Since He who walks on the sea is here.

V.

Peter, Peter! He does not speak;
　He is not as rash as in old Galilee:
Safer a ship, though it toss and leak,
　Than a reeling foot on a rolling sea!
　And he's got to be round in the girth, thinks he.

VI.

Peter, Peter! He does not stir;
　His nets are heavy with silver fish;
He reckons his gains, and is keen to infer
　—'The broil on the shore, if the Lord should wish;
　But the sturgeon goes to the Cæsar's dish.'

VII.

Peter, Peter! thou fisher of men,
　Fisher of fish wouldst thou live instead?
Haggling for pence with the other Ten,
　Cheating the market at so much a head,
　Griping the Bag of the traitor Dead?

VIII.

At the triple crow of the Gallic cock
   Thou weep'st not, thou, though thine eyes be dazed :
What bird comes next in the tempest-shock ?
   —Vultures ! see,—as when Romulus gazed,—
To inaugurate Rome for a world amazed !

THE KING'S GIFT.

I.

TERESA, ah, Teresita!
Now what has the messenger brought her,
Our Garibaldi's young daughter,
    To make her stop short in her singing?
Will she not once more repeat a
Verse from that hymn of our hero's,
    Setting the souls of us ringing?
Break off the song where the tear rose?
    Ah, Teresita!

II.

A young thing, mark, is Teresa:
Her eyes have caught fire, to be sure, in
That necklace of jewels from Turin,
    Till blind their regard to us men is.
But still she remembers to raise a
Sly look to her father, and note—
    'Could she sing on as well about Venice,
Yet wear such a flame at her throat?
    Decide for Teresa.'

III.

Teresa! ah, Teresita!
His right hand has paused on her head—
'Accept it, my daughter,' he said;
  'Ay, wear it, true child of thy mother!
Then sing, till all start to their feet, a
New verse ever bolder and freer!
  King Victor's no king like another,
But verily noble as *we* are,
    Child, Teresita!'

PARTING LOVERS.

SIENA, 1860.

— ♦ —

I.

I LOVE thee, love thee, Giulio;
  Some call me cold, and some demure;
And if thou hast ever guessed that so
  I loved thee . . well, the proof was poor,
    And no one could be sure.

II.

Before thy song (with shifted rhymes
  To suit my name) did I undo
The persian?   If it stirred sometimes,
  Thou hast not seen a hand push through
    A foolish flower or two.

III.

My mother listening to my sleep,
  Heard nothing but a sigh at night,—
The short sigh rippling on the deep,
  When hearts run out of breath and sight
    Of men, to God's clear light.

IV.

When others named thee,—thought thy brows
    Were straight, thy smile was tender,—'Here
He comes between the vineyard-rows!'
    I said not 'Ay,' nor waited, Dear,
        To feel thee step too near.

V.

I left such things to bolder girls,—
    Olivia or Clotilda.   Nay,
When that Clotilda, through her curls,
    Held both thine eyes in hers one day,
        I marvelled, let me say.

VI.

I could not try the woman's trick :
    Between us straightway fell the blush
Which kept me separate, blind and sick.
    A wind came with thee in a flush,
        As blown through Sinai's bush.

VII.

But now that Italy invokes
    Her young men to go forth and chase
The foe or perish,—nothing chokes
    My voice, or drives me from the place.
        I look thee in the face.

VIII.

I love thee! It is understood,
  Confest: I do not shrink or start.
No blushes! all my body's blood
  Has gone to greaten this poor heart,
    That, loving, we may part.

IX.

Our Italy invokes the youth
  To die if need be. Still there's room,
Though earth is strained with dead in truth:
  Since twice the lilies were in bloom
    They have not grudged a tomb.

X.

And many a plighted maid and wife
  And mother, who can say since then
'My country,'—cannot say through life
  'My son,' 'my spouse,' 'my flower of men,'
    And not weep dumb again.

XI.

Heroic males the country bears,—
  But daughters give up more than sons:
Flags wave, drums beat, and unawares
  You flash your souls out with the guns,
    And take your Heaven at once.

XII.

But we !—we empty heart and home
  Of life's life, love ! We bear to think
You're gone,—to feel you may not come,—
  To hear the door-latch stir and clink,
    Yet no more you ! . . nor sink.

XIII.

Dear God ! when Italy is one,
  Complete, content from bound to bound,
Suppose, for my share, earth 's undone
  By one grave in 't !—as one small wound
    Will kill a man, 'tis found.

XIV.

What then ? If love's delight must end,
  At least we 'll clear its truth from flaws.
I love thee, love thee, sweetest friend !
  Now take my sweetest without pause,
    And help the nation's cause.

XV.

And thus, of noble Italy
  We 'll both be worthy ! Let her show
The future how we made her free,
  Not sparing life . . nor Giulio,
    Nor this . . this heartbreak ! Go.

MOTHER AND POET.

TURIN, AFTER NEWS FROM GAETA, 1861.

I.

DEAD! One of them shot by the sea in the east,
  And one of them shot in the west by the sea.
Dead! both my boys! When you sit at the feast
  And are wanting a great song for Italy free,
    Let none look at *me!*

II.

Yet I was a poetess only last year,
  And good at my art, for a woman, men said;
But *this* woman, *this*, who is agonized here,
  —The east sea and west sea rhyme on in her head
    For ever instead.

III.

What art can a woman be good at? Oh, vain!
  What art *is* she good at, but hurting her breast
With the milk-teeth of babes, and a smile at the pain?
  Ah boys, how you hurt! you were strong as you pressed,
    And I proud, by that test.

IV.

What art's for a woman? To hold on her knees
   Both darlings! to feel all their arms round her throat,
Cling, strangle a little! to sew by degrees
   And 'broider the long-clothes and neat little coat;
      To dream and to doat.

V.

To teach them . . It stings there! *I* made them indeed
   Speak plain the word *country*. *I* taught them, no doubt,
That a country's a thing men should die for at need.
   I prated of liberty, rights, and about
      The tyrant cast out.

VI.

And when their eyes flashed . . O my beautiful eyes! . .
   I exulted; nay, let them go forth at the wheels
Of the guns, and denied not.   But then the surprise
   When one sits quite alone!   Then one weeps, then one
         kneels!
      God, how the house feels!

VII.

At first, happy news came, in gay letters moiled
   With my kisses,—of camp-life and glory, and how
They both loved me; and, soon coming home to be spoiled,
   In return would fan off every fly from my brow
      With their green laurel-bough.

VIII.

Then was triumph at Turin: 'Ancona was free!'
    And some one came out of the cheers in the street,
With a face pale as stone, to say something to me.
    My Guido was dead! I fell down at his feet,
        While they cheered in the street.

IX.

I bore it; friends soothed me; my grief looked sublime
    As the ransom of Italy. One boy remained
To be leant on and walked with, recalling the time
    When the first grew immortal, while both of us strained
        To the height he had gained.

X.

And letters still came, shorter, sadder, more strong,
    Writ now but in one hand, 'I was not to faint,—
One loved me for two—would be with me ere long:
    And *Viva l'Italia!—he* died for, our saint,
        Who forbids our complaint.'

XI.

My Nanni would add, 'he was safe, and aware
    Of a presence that turned off the balls,—was imprest
It was Guido himself, who knew what I could bear,
    And how 'twas impossible, quite dispossessed,
        To live on for the rest.'

XII.

On which, without pause, up the telegraph-line
　　Swept smoothly the next news from Gaeta :—*Shot.*
Tell his mother. Ah, ah, ' his,' ' their ' mother,—not ' mine,'
　　No voice says ' *My* mother' again to me. What !
　　　　You think Guido forgot ?

XIII.

Are souls straight so happy that, dizzy with Heaven,
　　They drop earth's affections, conceive not of woe ?
I think not. Themselves were too lately forgiven
　　Through THAT Love and Sorrow which reconciled so
　　　　The Above and Below.

XIV.

O Christ of the five wounds, who look'dst through the dark
　　To the face of Thy mother ! consider, I pray,
How we common mothers stand desolate, mark,
　　Whose sons, not being Christs, die with eyes turned away,
　　　　And no last word to say !

XV.

Both boys dead ? but that's out of nature. We all
　　Have been patriots, yet each house must always keep one.
'Twere imbecile, hewing out roads to a wall ;
　　And, when Italy's made, for what end is it done
　　　　If we have not a son ?

XVI.

Ah, ah, ah! when Gaeta's taken, what then?
　　When the fair wicked queen sits no more at her sport
Of the fire-balls of death crashing souls out of men?
　　When the guns of Cavalli with final retort
　　　　Have cut the game short?

XVII.

When Venice and Rome keep their new jubilee,
　　When your flag takes all heaven for its white, green and
　　　　red,
When *you* have your country from mountain to sea,
　　When King Victor has Italy's crown on his head,
　　　　(And *I* have my Dead)—

XVIII.

What then? Do not mock me. Ah, ring your bells low,
　　And burn your lights faintly! *My* country is *there*,
Above the star pricked by the last peak of snow:
　　My Italy's THERE, with my brave civic Pair,
　　　　To disfranchise despair!

XIX.

Forgive me. Some women bear children in strength,
　　And bite back the cry of their pain in self-scorn;
But the birth-pangs of nations will wring us at length
　　Into wail such as this—and we sit on forlorn
　　　　When the man-child is born.

XX.

Dead! One of them shot by the sea in the east,
   And one of them shot in the west by the sea.
Both! both my boys! If in keeping the feast
   You want a great song for your Italy free,
      Let none look at *me*!

[This was Laura Savio, of Turin, a poetess and patriot, whose sons
were killed at Ancona and Gaeta.]

NATURE'S REMORSES.

ROME, 1861.

—◆·

I.

HER soul was bred by a throne, and fed
  From the sucking-bottle used in her race
    On starch and water (for mother's milk
Which gives a larger growth instead),
  And, out of the natural liberal grace,
    Was swaddled away in violet silk.

II.

And young and kind, and royally blind,
  Forth she stepped from her palace-door
    On three-piled carpet of compliments,
Curtains of incense drawn by the wind
  In between her for evermore
    And daylight issues of events.

III.

On she drew, as a queen might do,
  To meet a Dream of Italy,—
    Of magical town and musical wave,

Where even a god, his amulet blue
 Of shining sea, in an ecstasy
  Dropt and forgot in a nereid's cave.

IV.

Down she goes, as the soft wind blows,
 To live more smoothly than mortals can,
  To love and to reign as queen and wife,
To wear a crown that smells of a rose,
 And still, with a sceptre as light as a fan,
  Beat sweet time to the song of life.

V.

What is this? As quick as a kiss
 Falls the smile from her girlish mouth!
  The lion-people has left its lair,
Roaring along her garden of bliss,
 And the fiery underworld of the South
  Scorched a way to the upper air.

VI.

And a fire-stone ran in the form of a man,
 Burningly, boundingly, fatal and fell,
  Bowling the kingdom down! Where was the king?
She had heard somewhat, since life began,
 Of terrors on earth and horrors in hell,
  But never, never of such a thing!

VII.

You think she dropped when her dream was stopped,
　　When the blotch of Bourbon blood inlay,
　　　　Lividly rank, her new lord's cheek?
Not so. Her high heart overtopped
　　The royal part she had come to play.
　　　　Only the men in that hour were weak.

VIII.

And twice a wife by her ravaged life,
　　And twice a queen by her kingdom lost,
　　　　She braved the shock and the counter-shock
Of hero and traitor, bullet and knife,
　　While Italy pushed, like a vengeful ghost,
　　　　That son of the Cursed from Gaeta's rock.

IX.

What will ye give her, who could not deliver,
　　German Princesses? A laurel-wreath
　　　　All over-scored with your signatures,
Graces, Serenities, Highnesses ever?
　　Mock her not, fresh from the truth of Death,
　　　　Conscious of dignities higher than yours.

X.

What will ye put in your casket shut,
　　Ladies of Paris, in sympathy's name?
　　　　Guizot's daughter, what have you brought her?

Withered immortelles, long ago cut
   For guilty dynasties perished in shame,
      Putrid to memory, Guizot's daughter?

XI.

Ah poor queen! so young and serene!
   What shall we do for her, now hope 's done,
      Standing at Rome in these ruins old,
She too a ruin and no more a queen?
   Leave her that diadem made by the sun
      Turning her hair to an innocent gold.

XII.

Ay! bring close to her, as 'twere a rose, to her,
   You free child from an Apennine city
      Singing for Italy,—dumb in the place!
Something like solace, let us suppose, to her
   Given, in that homage of wonder and pity,
      By his pure eyes to her beautiful face.

XIII.

Nature, excluded, savagely brooded,
   Ruined all queendom and dogmas of state,—
      Then in reaction remorseful and mild,
Rescues the womanhood, nearly eluded,
   Shows her what's sweetest in womanly fate—
      Sunshine from Heaven, and the eyes of a child.

THE NORTH AND THE SOUTH.

[THE LAST POEM.]

ROME, MAY, 1861.

—◆—

I.

'Now give us lands where the olives grow,'
    Cried the North to the South,
'Where the sun with a golden mouth can blow
Blue bubbles of grapes down a vineyard-row!'
    Cried the North to the South.

'Now give us men from the sunless plain,'
    Cried the South to the North,
'By need of work in the snow and the rain,
Made strong, and brave by familiar pain!'
    Cried the South to the North.

II.

'Give lucider hills and intenser seas,'
    Said the North to the South,
'Since ever by symbols and bright degrees
Art, childlike, climbs to the dear Lord's knees,'
    Said the North to the South.

'Give strenuous souls for belief and prayer,'
    Said the South to the North,
'That stand in the dark on the lowest stair,
While affirming of God, ' He is certainly there,' '
    Said the South to the North.

III.

'Yet oh, for the skies that are softer and higher !'
    Sighed the North to the South ;
'For the flowers that blaze, and the trees that aspire,
And the insects made of a song or a fire !'
    Sighed the North to the South.

'And oh, for a seer to discern the same !'
    Sighed the South to the North ;
'For a poet's tongue of baptismal flame,
To call the tree or the flower by its name !'
    Sighed the South to the North.

IV.

The North sent therefore a man of men
    As a grace to the South ;
And thus to Rome came Andersen.
—" *Alas, but must you take him again ?*'
    Said the South to the North.

TRANSLATIONS.

PARAPHRASE ON THEOCRITUS.

————◆————

THE CYCLOPS.

(Idyll XI.)

AND so an easier life our Cyclops drew,
  The ancient Polyphemus, who in youth
Loved Galatea while the manhood grew
  Adown his cheeks and darkened round his mouth.
No jot he cared for apples, olives, roses ;
  Love made him mad : the whole world was neglected,
The very sheep went backward to their closes
  From out the fair green pastures, self-directed.
    And singing Galatea, thus, he wore
    The sunrise down along the weedy shore,
And pined alone, and felt the cruel wound
  Beneath his heart, which Cypris' arrow bore,
With a deep pang ; but, so, the cure was found ;
    And sitting on a lofty rock he cast
    His eyes upon the sea, and sang at last :—

"O whitest Galatea, can it be
  That thou shouldst spurn me off who love thee so ?

More white than curds, my girl, thou art to see,
More meek than lambs, more full of leaping glee
    Than kids, and brighter than the early glow
On grapes that swell to ripen,—sour like thee!
Thou comest to me with the fragrant sleep,
    And with the fragrant sleep thou goest from me;
Thou fliest . . fliest, as a frightened sheep
    Flies the grey wolf!—yet Love did overcome me,
So long;—I loved thee, maiden, first of all
    When down the hills (my mother fast beside thee)
I saw thee stray to pluck the summer-fall
    Of hyacinth bells, and went myself to guide thee:
And since my eyes have seen thee, they can leave thee
    No more, from that day's light!   But thou . . by Zeus,
Thou wilt not care for *that*, to let it grieve thee!
    I know thee, fair one, why thou springest loose
From my arm round thee.   Why?   I tell thee, Dear!
    One shaggy eyebrow draws its smudging road
Straight through my ample front, from ear to ear,—
    One eye rolls underneath; and yawning, broad
Flat nostrils feel the bulging lips too near.
Yet . . ho, ho!—*I*,—whatever I appear,—
    Do feed a thousand oxen!   When I have done,
I milk the cows, and drink the milk that's best!
    I lack no cheese, while summer keeps the sun;
And after, in the cold, it's ready prest!
    And then, I know to sing, as there is none
Of all the Cyclops can, . . a song of thee,
Sweet apple of my soul, on love's fair tree,
And of myself who love thee . . till the West
Forgets the light, and all but I have rest.

I feed for thee, besides, eleven fair does,
    And all in fawn; and four tame whelps of bears.
Come to me, Sweet! thou shalt have all of those
    In change for love! I will not halve the shares.
Leave the blue sea, with pure white arms extended
    To the dry shore; and, in my cave's recess,
Thou shalt be gladder for the noonlight ended,—
    For here be laurels, spiral cypresses,
Dark ivy, and a vine whose leaves enfold
Most luscious grapes; and here is water cold,
    The wooded Ætna pours down through the trees
From the white snows,—which gods were scarce too bold
    To drink in turn with nectar. Who with these
Would choose the salt wave of the lukewarm seas?
Nay, look on me! If I am hairy and rough,
    I have an oak's heart in me; there's a fire
In these grey ashes which burns hot enough;
    And when I burn for *thee*, I grudge the pyre
No fuel . . not my soul, nor this one eye,—
Most precious thing I have, because thereby
I see thee, Fairest! Out, alas! I wish
My mother had borne me finned like a fish,
That I might plunge down in the ocean near thee,
    And kiss thy glittering hand between the weeds,
If still thy face were turned; and I would bear thee
    Each lily white, and poppy fair that bleeds
Its red heart down its leaves!—one gift, for hours
    Of summer, . . one, for winter; since, to cheer thee,
I could not bring at once all kinds of flowers.
Even now, girl, now, I fain would learn to swim,
    If stranger in a ship sailed nigh, I wis,—

That I may know how sweet a thing it is
To live down with you, in the Deep and Dim!
Come up, O Galatea, from the ocean,
      And having come, forget again to go!
As I, who sing out here my heart's emotion,
      Could sit for ever.   Come up from below!
Come, keep my flocks beside me, milk my kine,—
      Come, press my cheese, distrain my whey and curd!
Ah, mother! she alone . . that mother of mine . .
      Did wrong me sore!   I blame her!—Not a word
Of kindly intercession did she address
Thine ear with for my sake; and ne'ertheless
      She saw me wasting, wasting, day by day!
      Both head and feet were aching, I will say,
All sick for grief, as I myself was sick!
      O Cyclops, Cyclops, whither hast thou sent
      Thy soul on fluttering wings?   If thou wert bent
On turning bowls, or pulling green and thick
      The sprouts to give thy lambkins,—thou wouldst make
        thee
      A wiser Cyclops than for what we take thee.
Milk dry the present!   Why pursue too quick
That future which is fugitive aright?
      Thy Galatea thou shalt haply find,—
      Or else a maiden fairer and more kind;
For many girls do call me through the night,
      And, as they call, do laugh out silverly.
      I, too, am something in the world, I see!"

While thus the Cyclops love and lambs did fold,
Ease came with song, he could not buy with gold.

PARAPHRASES ON APULEIUS.

◆

PSYCHE GAZING ON CUPID.

(METAMORPH., Lib. IV.)

THEN Psyche, weak in body and soul, put on
 The cruelty of Fate, in place of strength :
She raised the lamp to see what should be done,
 And seized the steel, and was a man at length
In courage, though a woman! Yes, but when
 The light fell on the bed whereby she stood
To view the ' *beast* ' that lay there,—certes, then,
 She saw the gentlest, sweetest beast in wood—
Even Cupid's self, the beauteous god! more beauteous
 For that sweet sleep across his eyelids dim !
The light, the lady carried as she viewed,
 Did blush for pleasure as it lighted him,
The dagger trembled from its aim unduteous ;
 And *she* . . oh, *she*—amazed and soul-distraught,
And fainting in her whiteness like a veil,
 Slid down upon her knees, and, shuddering, thought

To hide—though in her heart—the dagger pale!
She would have done it, but her hands did fail
  To hold the guilty steel, they shivered so,—
And feeble, exhausted, unawares she took
To gazing on the god,—till, look by look,
  Her eyes with larger life did fill and glow.
She saw his golden head alight with curls,—
    She might have guessed their brightness in the dark
    By that ambrosial smell of heavenly mark!
She saw the milky brow, more pure than pearls,
    The purple of the cheeks, divinely sundered
By the globed ringlets, as they glided free,
Some back, some forwards,—all so radiantly,
    That, as she watched them there, she never wondered
    To see the lamplight, where it touched them, tremble:
On the god's shoulders, too, she marked his wings
    Shine faintly at the edges and resemble
A flower that's near to blow.   The poet sings
    And lover sighs, that Love is fugitive;
And certes, though these pinions lay reposing,
    The feathers on them seemed to stir and live
As if by instinct, closing and unclosing.
    Meantime the god's fair body slumbered deep,
    All worthy of Venus, in his shining sleep;
    While at the bed's foot lay the quiver, bow,
And darts,—his arms of godhead.   Psyche gazed
    With eyes that drank the wonders in,—said,—"Lo,
Be these my husband's arms?"—and straightway raised
    An arrow from the quiver-case, and tried
Its point against her finger,—trembling till

She pushed it in too deeply (foolish bride!)
And made her blood some dewdrops small distil,
And learnt to love Love, of her own goodwill.

—

PSYCHE WAFTED BY ZEPHYRUS.

(METAMORPH., Lib. IV.)

WHILE Psyche wept upon the rock forsaken,
   Alone, despairing, dreading,—gradually
By Zephyrus she was enwrapt and taken
   Still trembling,—like the lilies planted high,—
Through all her fair white limbs.   Her vesture spread,
   Her very bosom eddying with surprise,—
He drew her slowly from the mountain-head,
   And bore her down the valleys with wet eyes,
And laid her in the lap of a green dell
   As soft with grass and flowers as any nest,
With trees beside her, and a limpid well:
   Yet Love was not far off from all that Rest.

PSYCHE AND PAN.

(Metamorph., Lib. V.)

The gentle River, in her Cupid's honour,
    Because he used to warm the very wave,
Did ripple aside, instead of closing on her,
    And cast up Psyche, with a refluence brave,
Upon the flowery bank,—all sad and sinning.
Then Pan, the rural god, by chance was leaning
    Along the brow of waters as they wound,
    Kissing the reed-nymph till she sank to ground,
And teaching, without knowledge of the meaning,
    To run her voice in music after his
Down many a shifting note; (the goats around,
    In wandering pasture and most leaping bliss,
Drawn on to crop the river's flowery hair.)
And as the hoary god beheld her there,
    The poor, worn, fainting Psyche!—knowing all
    The grief she suffered, he did gently call
Her name, and softly comfort her despair :—

    "O wise, fair lady, I am rough and rude,
And yet experienced through my weary age!
    And if I read aright, as soothsayer should,
Thy faltering steps of heavy pilgrimage,

Thy paleness, deep as snow we cannot see
The roses through,—thy sighs of quick returning,
Thine eyes that seem, themselves, two souls in mourning,—
　　Thou lovest, girl, too well, and bitterly!
But hear me: rush no more to a headlong fall:
　　Seek no more deaths! leave wail, lay sorrow down,
And pray the sovran god; and use withal
　　Such prayer as best may suit a tender youth,
Well-pleased to bend to flatteries from thy mouth
　　And feel them stir the myrtle of his crown."

—So spake the shepherd-god; and answer none
Gave Psyche in return: but silently
She did him homage with a bended knee,
　　And took the onward path.—

PSYCHE PROPITIATING CERES.

(METAMORPH., Lib. VI.)

THEN mother Ceres from afar beheld her,
　　While Psyche touched, with reverent fingers meek,
The temple's scythes; and with a cry compelled her:—
　　"O wretched Psyche, Venus roams to seek
Thy wandering footsteps round the weary earth,
Anxious and maddened, and adjures thee forth
　　To accept the imputed pang, and let her wreak

I

Full vengeance with full force of deity!
    Yet *thou*, forsooth, art in my temple here,
Touching my scythes, assuming my degree,
    And daring to have thoughts that are not fear!"
—But Psyche clung to her feet, and as they moved
    Rained tears along their track, tear, dropped on tear,
And drew the dust on in her trailing locks,
    And still, with passionate prayer, the charge disproved:—
" Now, by thy right hand's gathering from the shocks
Of golden corn,—and by thy gladsome rites
Of harvest,—and thy consecrated sights
Shut safe and mute in chests,—and by the course
Of thy slave-dragons,—and the driving force
Of ploughs along Sicilian glebes profound,—
By thy swift chariot,—by thy steadfast ground,—
By all those nuptial torches that departed
    With thy lost daughter,—and by those that shone
Back with her, when she came again glad-hearted,—
    And by all other mysteries which are done
In silence at Eleusis,—I beseech thee,
    O Ceres, take some pity, and abstain
    From giving to my soul extremer pain
Who am the wretched Psyche! Let me teach thee
    A little mercy, and have thy leave to spend
A few days only in thy garnered corn,
    Until that wrathful goddess, at the end,
Shall feel her hate grow mild, the longer borne,—
Or till, alas!—this faintness at my breast
    Pass from me, and my spirit apprehend
From life-long woe a breath-time hour of rest!"

—But Ceres answered, "I am moved indeed
  By prayers so moist with tears, and would defend
The poor beseecher from more utter need :
  But where old oaths, anterior ties, commend,
  I cannot fail to a sister, lie to a friend,
As Venus is to *me*.   Depart with speed !"

PSYCHE AND THE EAGLE.

(METAMORPH., Lib. VI.)

But sovran Jove's rapacious Bird, the regal
High percher on the lightning, the great eagle
Drove down with rushing wings ; and,—thinking how,
By Cupid's help, he bore from Ida's brow
A cup-boy for his master,—he inclined
To yield, in just return, an influence kind ;
The god being honoured in his lady's woe.
And thus the Bird wheeled downward from the track,
Gods follow gods in, to the level low
Of that poor face of Psyche left in wrack.
—"Now fie, thou simple girl !" the Bird began ;
" For if thou think to steal and carry back
A drop of holiest stream that ever ran,
No simpler thought, methinks, were found in man.
What ! know'st thou not these Stygian waters be
Most holy, even to Jove ? that as, on earth,

Men swear by gods, and by the thunder's worth,
Even so the heavenly gods do utter forth
Their oaths by Styx's flowing majesty?
And yet, one little urnful, I agree
To grant thy need!" Whereat, all hastily,
He takes it, fills it from the willing wave,
And bears it in his beak, incarnadined
By the last Titan-prey he screamed to have;
And, striking calmly out, against the wind,
Vast wings on each side,—there, where Psyche stands,
He drops the urn down in her lifted hands.

PSYCHE AND CERBERUS.

(Metamorph., Lib. VI.)

A MIGHTY dog with three colossal necks,
    And heads in grand proportion; vast as fear,
With jaws that bark the thunder out that breaks
    In most innocuous dread for ghosts anear,
Who are safe in death from sorrow : he reclines
Across the threshold of queen Proserpine's
Dark-sweeping halls, and, there, for Pluto's spouse,
Doth guard the entrance of the empty house.
When Psyche threw the cake to him, once amain
He howled up wildly from his hunger-pain,
And was still, after.—

PSYCHE AND PROSERPINE.

(METAMORPH., Lib. VI.)

THEN Psyche entered in to Proserpine
In the dark house, and straightway did decline
With meek denial the luxurious seat,
   The liberal board for welcome strangers spread,
But sate down lowly at the dark queen's feet,
   And told her tale, and brake her oaten bread.
And when she had given the pyx in humble duty,
   And told how Venus did entreat the queen
To fill it up with only one day's beauty
   She used in Hades, star-bright and serene,
To beautify the Cyprian, who had been
   All spoilt with grief in nursing her sick boy,—
Then Proserpine, in malice and in joy,
   Smiled in the shade, and took the pyx, and put
   A secret in it; and so, filled and shut,
   Gave it again to Psyche. Could she tell
   It held no beauty, but a dream of hell?

PSYCHE AND VENUS.

(METAMORPH., Lib. VI.)

AND Pysche brought to Venus what was sent
By Pluto's spouse ; the paler, that she went
So low to seek it, down the dark descent.

MERCURY CARRIES PSYCHE TO OLYMPUS.

(METAMORPH., Lib. VI.)

THEN Jove commanded the god Mercury
To float up Psyche from the earth.   And she
Sprang at the first word, as the fountain springs,
And shot up bright and rustling through his wings.

MARRIAGE OF PSYCHE AND CUPID.

(METAMORPH., Lib. VI.)

AND Jove's right-hand approached the ambrosial bowl
    To Psyche's lips, that scarce dared yet to smile,—
" Drink, O my daughter, and acquaint thy soul
    With deathless uses, and be glad the while !
No more shall Cupid leave thy lovely side ;
    Thy marriage-joy begins for never-ending."
While yet he spake,— the nuptial feast supplied,—
    The bridegroom on the festive couch was bending
O'er Psyche in his bosom—Jove, the same,
    On Juno, and the other deities,
Alike ranged round.   The rural cup-boy came
    And poured Jove's nectar out with shining eyes,
While Bacchus, for the others, did as much,
    And Vulcan spread the meal ; and all the Hours
Made all things purple with a sprinkle of flowers,
Or roses chiefly, not to say the touch
    Of their sweet fingers ; and the Graces glided
Their balm around, and the Muses, through the air,
    Struck out clear voices, which were still divided
By that divinest song Apollo there
    Intoned to his lute ; while Aphroditè fair
Did float her beauty along the tune, and play
    The notes right with her feet.   And thus, the day

Through every perfect mood of joy was carried.
The Muses sang their chorus ; Satyrus
Did blow his pipes ; Pan touched his reed ;—and thus
At last were Cupid and his Psyche married.

PARAPHRASES ON NONNUS.

———◆———

HOW BACCHUS FINDS ARIADNE SLEEPING.

(Dionysiaca, Lib. XLVII.)

WHEN Bacchus first beheld the desolate
And sleeping Ariadne, wonder straight
Was mixed with love in his great golden eyes;
He turned to his Bacchantes in surprise,
And said with guarded voice,—"Hush! strike no more
Your brazen cymbals; keep those voices still
Of voice and pipe; and since ye stand before
Queen Cypris, let her slumber as she will!
And yet the cestus is not here in proof.
A Grace, perhaps, whom sleep has stolen aloof:
In which case, as the morning shines in view,
Wake this Aglaia!—yet in Naxos, who
Would veil a Grace so? Hush! And if that she
Were Hebe, which of all the gods can be
The pourer-out of wine? or if we think
She's like the shining moon by ocean's brink,

The guide of herds,—why, could she sleep without
Endymion's breath on her cheek? or if I doubt
Of silver-footed Thetis, used to tread
These shores,—even *she* (in reverence be it said)
Has no such rosy beauty to dress deep
With the blue waves.   The Loxian goddess might
Repose so from her hunting-toil aright
Beside the sea, since toil gives birth to sleep,
But who would find her with her tunic loose,
Thus?   Stand off, Thracian! stand off! Do not leap,
Not this way!   Leave that piping, since I choose,
O dearest Pan, and let Athené rest!
And yet if she be Pallas . . truly guessed . .
Her lance is—where? her helm and ægis—where?"
—As Bacchus closed, the miserable Fair
Awoke at last, sprang upward from the sands,
And gazing wild on that wild throng that stands
Around, around her, and no Theseus there!—
Her voice went moaning over shore and sea,
Beside the halcyon's cry; she called her love;
She named her hero, and raged maddeningly
Against the brine of waters; and above,
Sought the ship's track, and cursed the hours she slept
And still the chiefest execration swept
Against queen Paphia, mother of the ocean;
And cursed and prayed by times in her emotion
The winds all round.   .   .   .   .

Her grief did make her glorious; her despair
Adorned her with its weight.   Poor wailing child!
She looked like Venus when the goddess smiled

At liberty of godship, debonair;
Poor Ariadne! and her eyelids fair
Hid looks beneath them lent her by Persuasion
And every Grace, with tears of Love's own passion.
She wept long; then she spake :—" Sweet sleep did come
While sweetest Theseus went. O, glad and dumb,
1 wish he had left me still! for in my sleep
I saw his Athens, and did gladly keep
My new bride-state within my Theseus' hall;
And heard the pomp of Hymen, and the call
Of ' Ariadne, Ariadne,' sung
In choral joy; and there, with joy I hung
Spring-blossoms round love's altar!—ay, and wore
A wreath myself; and felt *him* evermore,
Oh, evermore beside me, with his mighty
Grave head bowed down in prayer to Aphroditè!
Why, what a sweet, sweet dream! *He* went with it,
And left me here unwedded where I sit!
Persuasion help me! The dark night did make me
    A brideship, the fair morning takes away;
My Love had left me when the Hour did wake me;
    And while I dreamed of marriage, as I say,
And blest it well, my blessèd Theseus left me:
And thus the sleep, 1 loved so, has bereft me.
Speak to me, rocks, and tell my grief to-day,
Who stole my love of Athens?" . . . .

HOW BACCHUS COMFORTS ARIADNE.

(DIONYSIACA, Lib. XLVII.)

THEN Bacchus' subtle speech her sorrow crossed :—
"O maiden, dost thou mourn for having lost
The false Athenian heart? and dost thou still
Take thought of Theseus, when thou may'st at will
Have Bacchus for a husband?   Bacchus bright!
A god in place of mortal!   Yes, and though
The mortal youth be charming in thy sight,
That man of Athens cannot strive below,
In beauty and valour, with my deity!
Thou'lt tell me of the labyrinthine dweller,
The fierce man-bull, he slew : I pray thee, be,
Fair Ariadne, the true deed's true teller,
And mention thy clue's help! because, forsooth,
Thine armed Athenian hero had not found
A power to fight on that prodigious ground,
Unless a lady in her rosy youth
Had lingered near him : not to speak the truth
Too definitely out till names be known—
Like Paphia's—Love's—and Ariadne's own.
Thou wilt not say that Athens can compare
With Æther, nor that Minos rules like Zeus,
Nor yet that Gnossus has such golden air
As high Olympus.   Ha! for noble use

We came to Naxos! Love has well intended
To change thy bridegroom! Happy thou, defended
From entering in thy Theseus' earthly hall,
That thou may'st hear the laughters rise and fall
Instead, where Bacchus rules! Or wilt thou choose
A still-surpassing glory?—take it all,—
A heavenly house, Kronion's self for kin,—
A place where Cassiopea sits within
Inferior light, for all her daughter's sake,
Since Perseus, even amid the stars, must take
Andromeda in chains aethereal!
But *I* will wreathe *thee*, sweet, an astral crown,
And as my queen and spouse thou shalt be known—
Mine, the crown-lover's!" Thus, at length, he proved
His comfort on her; and the maid was moved;
And casting Theseus' memory down the brine,
She straight received the troth of her divine
Fair Bacchus; Love stood by to close the rite:
The marriage-chorus struck up clear and light,
Flowers sprouted fast about the chamber green,
And with spring-garlands on their heads, I ween,
The Orchomenian dancers came along
And danced their rounds in Naxos to the song.
A Hamadryad sang a nuptial dit
Right shrilly: and a Naiad sate beside
A fountain, with her bare foot shelving it,
And hymned of Ariadne, beauteous bride,
Whom thus the god of grapes had deified.
Ortygia sang out, louder than her wont,
An ode which Phœbus gave her to be tried,
And leapt in chorus, with her steadfast front,

While prophet Love, the stars have called a brother,
Burnt in his crown, and twined in one another
His love-flower with the purple roses, given
In type of that new crown assigned in heaven.

PARAPHRASE ON HESIOD.

BACCHUS AND ARIADNE.

(THEOG. 947.)

THE golden-hairëd Bacchus did espouse
　　That fairest Ariadne, Minos' daughter,
And made her wifehood blossom in the house;
　　Where such protective gifts Kronion brought her,
Nor Death nor Age could find her when they sought her.

PARAPHRASE ON EURIPIDES.

————◆————

ANTISTROPHE.

(TROADES, 853.*)

LOVE, Love, who once didst pass the Dardan portals,
　　Because of Heavenly passion!
Who once didst lift up Troy in exultation,
To mingle in thy bond the high Immortals!—
　　　　Love, turned from his own name
　　　　　　To Zeus's shame,
　　　　　Can help no more at all.
And Eos' self, the fair, white-steeded Morning,—
Her light which blesses other lands, returning,
　　Has changed to a gloomy pall!
She looked across the land with eyes of amber,—
　　　　She saw the city's fall,—
　　　　She, who, in pure embraces,
Had held there, in the hymeneal chamber,
Her children's father, bright Tithonus old,
Whom the four steeds with starry brows and paces
Bore on, snatched upward, on the car of gold,
And with him, all the land's full hope of joy!
The love-charms of the gods are vain for Troy.

NOTE.—Rendered after Mr. Burges' reading, in some respects—not
quite all.

PARAPHRASES ON HOMER.

HECTOR AND ANDROMACHE.

(ILIAD, Lib. VI.)

SHE rushed to meet him: the nurse following
Bore on her bosom the unsaddened child,
A simple babe, prince Hector's well-loved son,
Like a star shining when the world is dark.
Scamandrius, Hector called him; but the rest
Named him Astyanax, the city's prince,
Because that Hector only, had saved Troy.
He, when he saw his son, smiled silently;
While, dropping tears, Andromache pressed on,
And clung to his hand, and spake, and named his name.

"Hector, my best one,—thine own nobleness
Must needs undo thee.   Pity hast thou none
For this young child, and this most sad myself,
Who soon shall be thy widow—since that soon
The Greeks will slay thee in the general rush—

And then, for me, what refuge, 'reft of *thee*,
But to go graveward?   Then, no comfort more
Shall touch me, as in the old sad times thou know'st—
Grief only—grief!   I have no father now,
No mother mild!   Achilles the divine,
He slew my father, sacked his lofty Thebes,
Cilicia's populous city, and slew its king,
Eëtion—father!—did not spoil the corse,
Because the Greek revered him in his soul,
But burnt the body with its dædal arms,
And poured the dust out gently.   Round that tomb
The Oreads, daughters of the goat-nursed Zeus,
Tripped in a ring, and planted their green elms.
There were seven brothers with me in the house,
Who all went down to Hades in one day,—
For *he* slew all, Achilles the divine,
Famed for his swift feet,—slain among their herds
Of cloven-footed bulls and flocking sheep!
My mother too, who queened it o'er the woods
Of Hippoplacia, he, with other spoil,
Seized,—and, for golden ransom, freed too late,—
Since, as she went home, arrowy Artemis
Met her and slew her at my father's door.
But—oh, my Hector,—thou art still to me
Father and mother!—yes, and brother dear,
O thou, who art my sweetest spouse beside!
Come now, and take me into pity!   Stay
I' the town here with us!   Do not make thy child
An orphan, nor a widow, thy poor wife!
Call up the people to the fig-tree, where

K

The city is most accessible, the wall
Most easy of assault!—for thrice thereby
The boldest Greeks have mounted to the breach,—
Both Ajaxes, the famed Idomeneus,
Two sons of Atreus, and the noble one
Of Tydeus,—whether taught by some wise seer,
Or by their own souls prompted and inspired."

Great Hector answered :—" Lady, for these things
It is my part to care.   And *I* fear most
My Trojans, and their daughters, and their wives,
Who through their long veils would glance scorn at me,
If, coward-like, I shunned the open war.
Nor doth my own soul prompt me to that end !
I learnt to be a brave man constantly,
And to fight foremost where my Trojans fight,
And vindicate my father's glory and mine—
Because I know, by instinct and my soul,
The day comes that our sacred Troy must fall,
And Priam and his people.   Knowing which,
I have no such grief for all my Trojans' sake,
For Hecuba's, for Priam's, our old king,
Not for my brothers', who so many and brave
Shall bite the dust before our enemies,—
As, sweet, for *thee !*—to think some mailèd Greek
Shall lead thee weeping and deprive thy life
Of the free sun-sight—that, when gone away
To Argos, thou shalt throw the distaff there
Not for thy uses—or shalt carry instead
Upon thy loathing brow, as heavy as doom,

The water of Greek wells—Messeis' own,
Or Hyperea's!—that some stander-by,
Marking thy tears fall, shall say, ' This is She,
The wife of that same Hector who fought best
Of all the Trojans, when all fought for Troy—'
Ay!—and, so speaking, shall renew thy pang
That, 'reft of Him so named, thou shouldst survive
To a slave's life!   But earth shall hide my corse
Ere that shriek sound, wherewith thou art dragged from
    Troy."

Thus Hector spake, and stretched his arms to his child.
Against the nurse's breast, with childly cry,
The boy clung back, and shunned his father's face,
And feared the glittering brass and waving hair
Of the high helmet, nodding horror down.
The father smiled, the mother could not choose
But smile too.   Then he lifted from his brow
The helm, and set it on the ground to shine :
Then, kissed his dear child—raised him with both arms,
And thus invoked Zeus and the general gods :—

" Zeus, and all godships ! grant this boy of mine
To be the Trojans' help, as I myself,—
To live a brave life and rule well in Troy !
Till men shall say, ' The son exceeds the sire
By a far glory.'   Let him bring home spoil
Heroic, and make glad his mother's heart."

With which prayer, to his wife's extended arms

He gave the child; and she received him straight
To her bosom's fragrance—smiling up her tears.
Hector gazed on her till his soul was moved;
Then softly touched her with his hand and spake.
" My best one—'ware of passion and excess
In any fear.   There's no man in the world
Can send me to the grave apart from fate,—
And no man . . Sweet, I tell thee . . can fly fate—
No good nor bad man.   Doom is self-fulfilled.
But now, go home, and ply thy woman's task
Of wheel and distaff! bid thy maidens haste
Their occupation.   War's a care for men—
For all men born in Troy, and chief for me."

Thus spake the noble Hector, and resumed
His crested helmet, while his spouse went home;
But as she went, still looked back lovingly,
Dropping the tears from her reverted face.

THE DAUGHTERS OF PANDARUS.

(ODYSS., Lib. XX.)

AND so these daughters fair of Pandarus,
The whirlwinds took.   The gods had slain their kin:
They were left orphans in their father's house.
And Aphroditè came to comfort them
With incense, luscious honey, and fragrant wine;

And Heré gave them beauty of face and soul
Beyond all women; purest Artemis
Endowed them with her stature and white grace;
And Pallas taught their hands to flash along
Her famous looms.   Then, bright with deity,
Toward far Olympus, Aphrodité went
To ask of Zeus (who has his thunder-joys
And his full knowledge of man's mingled fate)
How best to crown those other gifts with love
And worthy marriage: but, what time she went,
The ravishing Harpies snatched the maids away,
And gave them up, for all their loving eyes,
To serve the Furies who hate constantly.

ANOTHER VERSION.

So the storms bore the daughters of Pandarus out into
thrall—
The gods slew their parents; the orphans were left in the
hall.
And there, came, to feed their young lives, Aphrodité divine,
With the incense, the sweet-tasting honey, the sweet-smell-
ing wine;
Heré brought them her wit above woman's, and beauty of
face;
And pure Artemis gave them her stature, that form might
have grace:

And Athenè instructed their hands in her works of renown;
Then, afar to Olympus, divine Aphroditè moved on :
To complete other gifts, by uniting each girl to a mate,
She sought Zeus, who has joy in the thunder and know-
    ledge of fate,
Whether mortals have good chance or ill ! But the Harpies
    alate
In the storm came, and swept off the maidens, and gave
    them to wait,
With that love in their eyes, on the Furies who constantly
    hate.

PARAPHRASE ON ANACREON.

—◆—

ODE TO THE SWALLOW.

Thou indeed, little Swallow,
A sweet yearly comer,
Art building a hollow
New nest every summer,
And straight dost depart
Where no gazing can follow,
Past Memphis, down Nile!
Ah! but Love all the while
Builds his nest in my heart,
Through the cold winter-weeks:
And as one Love takes flight,
Comes another, O Swallow,
In an egg warm and white,
And another is callow.
And the large gaping beaks
Chirp all day and all night:
And the Loves who are older

Help the young and the poor Loves,
And the young Loves grown bolder
Increase by the score Loves—
Why, what can be done?
If a noise comes from one,
Can I bear all this rout of a hundred and more Loves?

PARAPHRASES ON HEINE.

———◆———

[THE LAST TRANSLATION.]

ROME, 1860.

I.

I.

OUT of my own great woe
I make my little songs,
Which rustle their feathers in throngs
And beat on her heart even so.

II.

They found the way, for their part,
Yet come again, and complain,
Complain, and are not fain
To say what they saw in her heart.

II.

I.

ART thou indeed so adverse ?
Art thou so changed indeed ?
Against the woman who wrongs me
I cry to the world in my need.

II.

O recreant lips unthankful,
How could ye speak evil, say,
Of the man who so well has kissed you
On many a fortunate day ?

III.

I.

MY child, we were two children,
Small, merry by childhood's law ;
We used to crawl to the hen-house
And hide ourselves in the straw.

II.

We crowed like cocks, and whenever
The passers near us drew—
Cock-a-doodle ! they thought
'Twas a real cock that crew.

III.

The boxes about our courtyard
We carpeted to our mind,
And lived there both together—
Kept house in a noble kind.

IV.

The neighbour's old cat often
Came to pay us a visit;
We made her a bow and curtsey,
Each with a compliment in it.

V.

After her health we asked,
Our care and regard to evince—
(We have made the very same speeches
To many an old cat since).

VI.

We also sate and wisely
Discoursed, as old folks do,
Complaining how all went better
In those good times we knew,—

VII.

How love and truth and believing
Had left the world to itself,
And how so dear was the coffee,
And how so rare was the pelf.

The children's games are over,
The rest is over with youth—
The world, the good games, the good times,
The belief, and the love, and the truth.

— ——

IV.

1.

THOU lovest me not, thou lovest me not!
   'Tis scarcely worth a sigh :
Let me look in thy face, and no king in his place
   Is a gladder man than I.

II.

Thou hatest me well, thou hatest me well—
   Thy little red mouth has told :
Let it reach me a kiss, and, however it is,
   My child, I am well consoled.

— ·—

V.

1.

MY own sweet Love, if thou in the grave,
   The darksome grave, wilt be,
Then will I go down by the side, and crave
   Love-room for thee and me.

II.

I kiss and caress and press thee wild,
　　Thou still, thou cold, thou white!
I wail, 1 tremble, and weeping mild,
　　Turn to a corpse at the right.

III.

The Dead stand up, the midnight calls,
　　They dance in airy swarms—
We two keep still where the grave-shade falls,
　　And I lie on in thine arms.

IV.

The Dead stand up, the Judgment-day
　　Bids such to weal or woe—
But nought shall trouble us where we stay
　　Embraced and embracing below.

VI.

I.

The years they come and go,
　　The races drop in the grave,
Yet never the love doth so,
　　Which here in my heart I have.

II.

Could I see thee but once, one day,
And sink down so on my knee,
And die in thy sight while I say,
'Lady, I love but thee!'

JOHN EDWARD TAYLOR, PRINTER,
LITTLE QUEEN STREET, LINCOLN'S INN FIELDS.

WORKS

BY

ELIZABETH BARRETT BROWNING.

—◆

ELIZABETH BARRETT BROWNING'S POETICAL WORKS.

FIFTH EDITION,

WITH CORRECTIONS AND ADDITIONS.

Three Vols. fcap. 8vo, cloth. 18s.

[*Published February, 1862.*]

AURORA LEIGH:

A POEM, IN NINE BOOKS.

FIFTH EDITION,

WITH PORTRAIT OF MRS. BROWNING.

One Vol. fcap. 8vo, cloth. 7s.

POEMS BEFORE CONGRESS.

Crown 8vo, cloth. 4s.

www.ingramcontent.com/pod-product-compliance
Lightning Source LLC
Chambersburg PA
CBHW021124020726
47500CB00003B/913